Bali OK

A Parable for a Changing Climate

Bali OK

A Parable for a Changing Climate

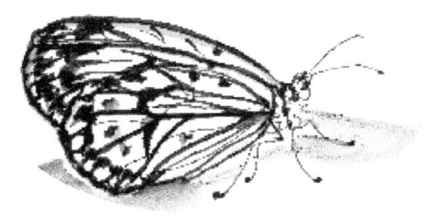

Carli Spero

To all our grandchildren

By finding small ways
to express appreciation for our planet,
we celebrate what we value.

The seed of all action is *Hope.*

— *Earth Logic*

"So, if you rape the earth, and *then* give it an
offering—does that make the earth a *prostitute*?"

— Cecily Palmera

Prelude

The flutter of a butterfly's wings *can* change the
course of global events . . .

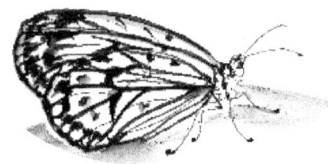

. . . *when the video goes viral.*

Chapter 1

Deborah leaned against the kitchen counter, checking her phone while she waited for the coffee to drip and the bread slices to toast. A lot, she could see, was happening on Pict. (This was the successor to Instagram, recently renamed to sound more permanent — kind of like a tattoo.)

There was an absolute *ton* of photos waiting for her. *Of course!* Cecily must be back from her honeymoon! She had obviously spent hours filtering and cropping. Her picture gallery reveled in a lush tropical background that put to shame those pathetic selfie stations that had become so popular in hotels and airports. Deborah was pleased to see, also, that the adorable newlyweds were not *always* holding drinks.

She perched on a kitchen stool and flipped through the romantic images, happy to see her niece looking so happy — sitting poolside, or shaded by a tree canopy, or geared up for snorkeling. But in the next moment, she stopped flipping through photos. Forgetting all about breakfast, she phoned her niece. *There was this photo of a butterfly.*

"Welcome home, sweet pea! I've been looking at your gallery on Pict!"

"Hey Aunt Deb! Please don't judge me, there's a couple hundred I *didn't* post."

"Not judging at all, just enjoying them. Listen, I'll be in New York next week. Can we have lunch? I want to hear about everything."

Deborah Morrison was a *lepidopterist*. At one time, when someone asked her what she did, she would simply lob that intimidating label into the conversation — and then enjoy watching the reaction, as people wondered whether this was maybe something they should worry about. These days, she would just answer the question directly: *I study butterflies*. It always felt a bit childish, though: butterflies had been her passion as a child, obsessively drawing and naming every butterfly she saw in a picture book. The same way — even today — she would have liked to sketch Cecily's winged friend, truth be told.

But by 2037, butterfly research was becoming a branch of extinction studies. There were almost no butterflies to be seen in people's gardens. Butterflies lived mainly in the tropical forests these days, and so that is where butterfly scientists went, too.

And this particular butterfly had been captured in a *honeymoon photo*!

Deborah examined the photo again. There was Cecily, seen in close-up, as she fake-smooched a small black-and-white butterfly that sat on her manicured left hand, helpfully showcasing the rings on her fourth finger. Its wings looked like a particularly delicate Art Deco stained glass.

In fact, there was something sweetly retro about Cecily's entire photo gallery. It had the sort of greenery and dappled sunlight that you saw in old family vacation photos. Everyone knew that beautiful lakes and whispering pines were, by now, iconic images of the past. You could still see such landscapes on greeting cards, but not so much on Pict and Gram, thanks to the ravages of tree borers and algae bloom. Even the most manicured landscaping was difficult to keep up, almost everywhere. If water was available, it was *too* plentiful. You were simply going to get dieback, whether from drought or root-rot.

But Cecily — now, this day — was posting the kinds of photos that her friends could have seen in their *parents'* honeymoon albums. And that was why Cecily's entire album quickly got labeled, on Pict, #honeymoonthrowback.

For Deborah, that butterfly photo was a revelation. This was *Ideopsis juventa juventa.* It used to be a very common rainforest butterfly — but, like so many others, it had suffered habitat loss for decades. And there was a bigger problem. Just like our own beloved Monarch butterfly, the "Wood Nymph" larvae depended on milkweed species as food. Although the milkweed's toxic compounds were harmless to the butterfly, they were not at all harmless to butterfly predators; weirdly, these butterflies were basically eating poison to protect themselves from their enemies. But of course, this meant that anything that affected the supply of milkweed would affect the butterfly.

Milkweed itself turned out to be a survivor. But by 2037, decades of ratcheting temperature and rainfall levels had the effect of diluting its toxicity, to the point that the larger tropical birds were generally safe from its effects. For these birds, the buffet was now set with a new food source — the delectable Wood Nymph butterfly. So, as Deborah was well aware, this butterfly had declined throughout Southeast Asia, almost to the point of extinction. Its decline was widely commented on: butterfly enthusiasts were worried that a similar fate could befall the Monarch butterfly. As northern regions shifted toward a more tropical climate, would our own milkweeds also lose their bite?

But here was this rare specimen of an endangered butterfly frolicking in Cecily's honeymoon album, far from any forest. The photo seemed to have been taken on the tiled patio of some hotel. On the island of Bali. Had butterflies survived in *hotels*?

Deborah's first thought was that perhaps some tropical milkweed varieties had adapted differently to the changed climate. She immediately sent out a query to the botanists in her consulting group. Two of them answered back, expressing their doubts about that theory.

Deborah's next thought was to check out climate patterns around Indonesia. But first, she had to pin down the location of this sighting. Where exactly was the photo taken? Not just the GPS coordinates, but details of the setting and the surrounding flora. Was it on a balcony? How high up? She needed all the details from Cecily. Next week, they would definitely have that lunch.

Chapter 2

Cecily's own job would have allowed a lot of flexibility, e-working from some nice location miles away from the city. But Mattias's IT job kept him in-office. She had no complaints, though; it felt rather special to be one of the New Yorkers who lived in town year-round, the way most of the arts community did. And she could easily carve out time to go out for lunch. Aunt Deb had agreed to meet at a grains-and-salad spot that had never heard of a "burger." (She would probably have drawn the line, though, Cecily guessed, at a grilled cricket lunch.)

Cecily scooped up her sidepack and her folding bike helmet (leaving behind the mini-canister of oxygen, which she only needed on Code Orange days), and she headed out of the building.

Pushing through the glass door of the Granary, Cecily immediately spotted her Aunt Deb. Plain glasses, throwback straight brown hair (that would no doubt be allowed to go gray someday), shirt buttoned more than most. Reading something, of course — not even on her phone, as if she actually belonged to an older generation. SO adorable! And simply gorgeous, if only she would agree to just a tiny makeover. . . .

Deborah stood up for a big hello hug, and they took their seats at the table.

"So. How does it feel to be *Mrs. Mattias Palmera?*"

"Aunt Deb, I am going to forgive you that 20th-century expression, just because everything is amazing. We are so happy, it feels like we've been together all our lives!"

But just as she said the word "lives," an unwelcome thought stifled her next words. Cecily saw, in that instant — actually, for the first time — that it was quite possible that her dear Aunt Deb would never, herself, be married. Cecily's gaze dropped to fix itself on the meaningless bunch of words on the menu. She wondered, all over again, what had gone wrong with Jason, and why the heck there wasn't anyone else.

(This was, of course, something Deborah had also asked herself, only about a million times. She would assure herself grimly — maybe while cutting up carrots, with a vengeance — "I *can so* laugh at myself!")

Looking up again, Cecily was relieved to see her Aunt Deb still beaming.

"And how was your fabulous week in Bali? I want all the details!"

Cecily was happy to relive her honeymoon: three perfect days relaxing at the beach, followed by four days surrounded by traditional Balinese culture, in historic Ubud. (She was careful to say the name properly: OO-bud.)

"We were wandering around Ubud on our first day, and some tourists told us there was a Hindu temple ceremony happening, just up the street! So we practically ran over there, and some people wrapped us in sarongs, right over our jeans, and some other people took us inside. There was this huge courtyard full of people, all sitting on the ground, all chanting and praying. There was even a dance performance! And nobody even asked us for money."

Cecily pulled out of her pack a souvenir for her favorite aunt — a brilliant green, gold-painted sarong.

And then, over her too-crunchy salad, Deborah began to explain her professional interest in *Ideopsis juventa juventa*.

"Seeing your close-up photo of the Wood Nymph butterfly almost knocked me off my seat! I never expected to see one of those — certainly not outside a rainforest."

"Well, I was pretty sure you would love seeing that butterfly, Aunt Deb," Cecily murmured, now staring fixedly at her quinoa bowl. "But I didn't know it would be *that* special." Honestly, she felt a bit deflated, not to be at the center of her own honeymoon. How did this woman-to-woman lunch suddenly become part of Aunt Deb's research? (Who, to be honest, never seemed all *that* excited about her wedding in the first place.)

Seeing the flash of irritation in Cecily's eyes, Deborah began to talk about the importance of species survival: almost as important as its survival is *knowing* that it survived. How completely fantastic, that Cecily had discovered a case where the "canary in the mine" seems to be okay! Cecily's smile came right back, bigger than before. She had personally found a thriving specimen of a doomed species. *And on her honeymoon!* What a perfect symbol for their marriage!

And that's why, as they were finishing their lunch, Cecily was already tweeting out that auspicious photo, using the hashtag "#**butterfly**okay." This was the shorthand people were using to tag any happy sign of climate normalcy. You could post a photo of Niagara Falls at full blast, with #**niagara**okay; or a picture of some redwoods that had been spared from California's droughts and wildfires, with #**redwood**okay; or even a view of a New York beach — a proud (if diminished) survivor of the erosion of the East Coast — with #**jonesbeach**okay. Everyone understood, of course, that "okay" was likely to be a relative (and possibly temporary) condition.

As they emerged into the shroud of heat, Deborah had an inspiration. "We should head up to 57th, for a gelato!" Cecily was way on board with that. Flipping up the pedals, she began to wheel her bike alongside as they walked.

"You know," Deborah recalled, "I was living not too far from here, back in the 2020s, during the virodemic. For a few months, it felt even emptier than this. No one went outside — ever — if they could stay inside."

"Is that when you were at the museum?"

"Um hm. Natural History. That was in the days when there was some research funding. I was working in the collection, and almost none of it had been digitized, so I was out of luck. They did bring me back six months later, to help with digitizing, and I could do my research again in my spare time."

They had stopped at the corner, and Deborah looked back at Cecily. "Your high school was closed for almost a year, right?"

"Yeah, we got so bored we started an online poker club. I never actually knew anyone who got sick though. Not personally." They started across the street. "It was my sister's class that got really screwed over, though."

"How is Meg doing?"

"She seems happy just being a mom. Mostly driving and baking, if you ask me."

After their gelatos and their goodbyes, it was Deborah's turn to jump onto her phone. Cecily had been happy to vouch for that photograph of the Wood Nymph butterfly, on the balcony of a hotel in Ubud; and now, with that confirmation, Deborah was ready to call in some expert guidance.

Stefan was the ideal person to go to with any new puzzle.

Stefan was Deborah's favorite colleague, specializing in butterfly research on the major islands of Indonesia and the southern Philippines. His boundless curiosity was coupled with scientific rigor. She vividly remembered one time when he spent several weeks investigating a news story about elephant language, and then was deeply shocked to find that no one seemed to care.

Yes, Stefan confirmed, Wood Nymphs could still be found. But he would have thought you'd have to trek into denser parts of the rainforest to see one. Unfortunately, just at the time when the study of butterflies was increasingly critical, it was attracting less research money. So, they were not going to find a robust catalog of field observations, either positive or negative. But just because there were no sightings did not mean that the butterflies had disappeared; actually, the field research had disappeared.

"Y'know, Deb, you just may have to do that field study yourself."

"But *someone* must have observed a Wood Nymph before now, if it's hanging around hotel balconies!"

This led Deborah to another thought: maybe the butterfly had a local name. Maybe someone in Bali might have posted something about it using their own vocabulary?

Stefan gave that suggestion a bit of thought. Since it was Bali, she might be in luck. There was a website called BasaBali (literally, "Balinese language") that had ballooned, wiki-style, over the past couple of decades. It was just possible that someone might have posted an item there on the Wood Nymph.

Frogs, like all amphibians, like to be in water. Even in a pot. On the stove. It is often remarked that if you want to boil a frog, just heat the water slowly enough and it won't even notice — it won't try to jump out of the pot until it's pretty much cooked. By 2037, of course, we were already living in Frogworld.

Cities were once again places to flee rather than flock to, much as in the days before air-conditioning. The rising CO_2, together with the heat ricocheting off sidewalks and buildings, made for an unpleasant environment for man and beast. People moved to places as leafy as they could afford. Suburbs were not as leafy as they used to be, of course, but there were still trees; people made a fetish of planting quick-growing species like willow oak. Anything that would add some green shade and take away some CO_2.

With the expansion of e-work, the idea of "suburbs" had become almost meaningless anyway. As long as you were working off-site, you might as well find a nice mountain retreat to call home.

Airlines proudly announced each minor fuel-saving innovation. One legacy airline had rebranded itself as Sol Air, through a flashy commercial partnership with the innovative solar battery manufacturer. Each of its planes had been retrofitted to carry the patented Sol "tray system," designed to charge several hundred batteries, high above the clouds.

The defiant hordes of Burning Man continued to populate the Nevada desert each August (!) — but now, they cavorted under huge, corporate-sponsored, super-cooled geodesic domes.

New apartment buildings all provided locked bicycle corrals.

The better-funded school districts were installing super-cooling systems, thereby giving their students an additional advantage.

Most online maps now showed sea level, as well as shoreline projections. News coverage, however, had retreated in the face of public exhaustion: all the day's disaster stories — all the epic floods and fires and migrations — were compiled into a daily squib, about the same the length as the horoscope.

Economic growth was a thing of the past. How are you going to grow an economy, when all the systems are in peril? Prediction, planning, and forecasting had become a matter of guesswork. Risk analysis? Not possible.

There were a few bits of good news. Surprisingly, cars: self-driving technologies, especially "super-look-ahead" capability, made driving so much smoother that even the old non-battery vehicles used less fuel. The new Sol batteries, pre-charged with solar power, could run anything from computers to coffeemakers, and the Sol re-charging stations for cars were popping up almost everywhere.

None of it was enough, of course. But for most people, it was just too depressing to think very much about where things were heading.

A couple of new professions had made a profitable niche for themselves. A *climate consultant* would find you a place to relocate to in the hot months. They could also facilitate an eco-coop membership, as a way to share the investment in supercooling or green technologies. The climate consultant would bring in *forecast specialists*, as needed, to assess the risk of extreme weather events for wherever you were planning to travel or relocate. They could also manage your carbon offsets for, say, travel and super cooling. It was not an easy job, but it paid very well — almost as much, per hour, as eco-anxiety therapy.

Many older Washingtonians disapproved of the new trend of planting tropical palm trees everywhere. They considered it Miamification — as if Miami was still its old boomingly vulgar self. (These folks were not necessarily "fossils," though some of them still wore ties and jackets — even in the summer.)

"Fossils" is the term for all the people who once insisted that things were fine when they weren't fine — a play, no doubt, on "fossil fuels." The remaining fossils naturally had their own theory about economic growth: women were simply not having enough children.

Manhattan real estate was completely seasonal now, like a kind of anti-resort. For the nearly six months of summer weather, people would relocate if they possibly could. After all, most people could do their work without being anywhere near the office. So, no one rented by the year anymore — they would rent for half-years. The bottom had fallen out of the real estate market some years ago, as Queens and Manhattan apartment prices began to converge. (Traffic jams? You're joking. Manhattan in summer looks almost as empty as it did during the 2020 virus pandemic.)

But if you did have to stay in Manhattan during the summer, the new "cooler collar" might help. It had a micro-Sol mechanism that worked by convection to extract body heat. It wasn't exactly a fashion statement: the thing looked a bit like those stiff white ruffs in a Dutch Masters painting. (Which, of course, were also functional — worn to keep the fleas from going above the wearer's neck.) The Moxy seemed to be catching on as well. This was a translucent oxygen-infused face mask, a device that perfectly completed the "alien harlequin" look.

Upstate New York, however, had revived, as the newest NYC suburb for monthly commuters. Cornell University dominated a good part of that landscape; and this was where Deborah's department was located, in the ever-valiant School of Agriculture. She felt fortunate to rent a comfortable apartment that was close enough to campus to be able to hear the famous clock tower chimes.

Chapter 3

The same week that Cecily was reveling in beautiful Bali, one Balinese agronomist was having something less of a honeymoon, in Malaysia.

Wayan Rawoh (WHY-an RAH-woe) had earned three professional degrees: two at the Balinese agricultural institute, and one at its Australian counterpart. He had become a widely respected go-to expert on rice irrigation in Bali. His expertise included the history and hydraulics of those incredibly photogenic ricefield terraces — a cultural phenomenon that had long been recognized (as he would proudly mention to any visitor) as a UNESCO World Heritage Site. Wayan was often sought out as a consultant on projects for USAID, the American international aid agency, as well as by other international development agencies, especially the Japanese and Swedish agencies.

But his own research absorbed most of his time and attention. For 20 years, Wayan had maintained a meticulous record of temperature and rainfall at six selected sites in Bali — two coastal, and four upland. He regularly uploaded his records into a database that was maintained (thanks to an ASEAN "climate grant") by a team of colleagues in Singapore. Their master database tracked average temperature and rainfall figures for locations in Malaysia, Philippines, Thailand, and Indonesia, going back between 10 and 20 years.

And now, he almost felt like throwing it all away.

Wayan was in Kuala Lumpur for the three-day biennial conference on Southeast Asian rice agriculture. It was held in the huge circular glass-enclosed auditorium that had been designed a decade ago, in a less eco-conscious era, to symbolize the transparency of scientific method. It always gave him the feeling that the scientists had somehow become the specimens.

This was his first opportunity to share his data beyond the working group of maybe a dozen colleagues, and his presentation would be an important contribution to the panel on rice irrigation. His main chart was a stunner. It captured two decades of data in a set of colored lines, showing the temperature trends for various Southeast Asian countries and regions. The orange line, representing Bali, showed a rise in temperature between 2020 and 2027, right in sync with the other lines — and then it launched itself back down, *retreating to the average levels of the previous decade.*

To be fair, Wayan had not encountered any actual hostility from the other scientists. But his presentation had generated only a few questions — all of them skeptical — and zero sustained interest. Even after the panel, there was no one asking for his report or even for his contact information; people had swooped right past him, to cluster around one or two of the other five presenters.

It was not just pride of authorship that told Wayan that his work was significant. His working group had highlighted his Balinese data as an area warranting further research. Three of them had actually traveled to Bali to accompany him on a monthly site visit; they had interviewed his assistants and even tested his digital protocols, instruments, and links. Wayan had welcomed their interest, and he had made sure to cite their summaries in his presentation.

The climatologist he had consulted with, who had helped design his monitoring setup in the first place, had himself been intrigued, and baffled, that the Balinese microclimate showed such stability. No matter how you charted the data, Bali was a meteorological outlier in Southeast Asia. And none of the larger meteorological factors — ocean currents, and equatorial winds — could account for this pattern.

Indeed, if Wayan had been at all inclined to share on social media, he might well have posted #**bali**okay.

But his target audience wasn't the twitter mob; it was his peers in agronomic science. And here, his work was being dismissed as at best a local anomaly, at worst an error of measurement. They apparently felt that it simply could not be true, that it was an exercise in wishful thinking. How, in the year 2037, could you have the *same* temperature and rainfall as in the 2020s?

Wayan slept badly that night, in his "Temporized" hotel room in KL. (Tempi Air was a greener technology than A/C.) He dreamed that he was watching the intricate stone carvings on his family's home shrine soften, dissolve, and lose their form, before gradually regaining their normal shapes. But then the six-foot-high stone shrine began to stretch itself higher and higher, becoming a pencil-like tower that leaned toward him.

And now, in his dream, there are two Balinese dancers — women — coming to place their small offering baskets. One reaches up to place her offering high on the temple ledge; the other dancer kneels down, to place her offering on the ground. But those offerings, too, were already dissolving in the women's hands.

Waking with a start, Wayan blinked the dream away.

His mind immediately jerked him back to his panel presentation — that painful silence when he finished, the lack of any interest in what he had to say. What could he have done differently? Maybe the problem was simply that his English wasn't good enough. Still too Australian, maybe? (The Interp.ret app had been set up, but he didn't trust it.) Would things have gone differently for him if the whole panel had been given in Indonesian?

Or, even, perhaps, in Balinese? It was an absurd idea. Must be an echo from that dream.

He would not even know how to frame his own work in Balinese. After all, he studies *water*. Of all the various terms for water in Balinese, none has the neutral tone of the English word. Balinese has words for water that flows, water that has been blessed, water to be thrown away. And then that thought melted into another random thought. The old Balinese religion is called *agama tirta*, the religion of sacred water. Could *that* have anything at all to do with the "water" he has studied for two decades?

Wayan gave himself a shake. He decided to post his chart of comparative temperatures, the very next morning, on the news page of the cultural wiki, BasaBali.

Deborah was facing some difficulties of her own, in trying to find a research grant to investigate *Ideopsis juventa juventa*. She knew better, of course, than to cite social media to document a sighting. And, unfortunately, none of the photos Cecily could provide show the kind of detail that a researcher would require. No one accused her of faking the photos, but the grant was not approved.

Fortunately, she was not teaching classes this summer. Deborah decided to take herself to the island of Bali.

Bali was a place that Deborah would never have considered for a vacation, even on the rare occasion when she took one. Bali was firmly associated with *honeymoons*: the trip ate up way too many airmiles for a conscientious New Yorker to travel on holiday. And for Deborah, that dreamy honeymoon aura was a bug and not a feature. It had been several years since she had any serious thought of planning her own honeymoon. But by now (she told herself), all that was in the rear-view mirror; she was well past thinking of her relationship with Jason as some sort of lost opportunity. She could travel wherever she needed to — and she'd find some way to offset those airmiles.

Her preliminary research on the elusive Wood Nymph was frustrating. She found no current reports of *Ideopsis* sightings (in any variant), but this was probably because — as Stefan had warned — the research resources just didn't exist. And even on that BasaBali wiki he had recommended, her diligent search on every conceivably related vocabulary item turned up no specific butterfly terms at all (apart from a delightful generic term, *kupu-kupu*).

But she did find something else there. On the main News page of the BasaBali website, someone had posted a chart showing average temperature trends for Southeast Asia, in selected locations. And even a glance at that chart showed that there was nothing normal about the trend for Bali. Or rather, the current Bali trend looked more like the "old normal" than the new normal.

Was it too great a stretch to think that this peculiar weather pattern could explain the sighting of a Wood Nymph butterfly on a hotel balcony in Ubud? And did it also explain why Cecily's honeymoon photos breathed of that green-filtered sunlight, a light that was as nostalgic, in its way, as a sepia-tinted portrait?

That temperature chart — along with the name of its author, Dr. Wayan Rawoh — was immediately entered into Deborah's research spreadsheet.

The email had to have the proper tone: a professional inquiry, directed to a potential research source (albeit in a completely different field). Judging from this climate chart, Dr. Rawoh's weather study represented the sort of ground-breaking research that would quickly attract both collaborators and timewasters, and Deborah was determined not to be lumped into the latter category. She wanted to come across as serious and respectful, providing enough background to establish her credibility, but not so much as to appear arrogant — especially in a cross-cultural communication.

Following Stefan's suggestion, Deborah had located an email address for Dr. Wayan Rawoh at the Bali Agricultural Institute. Hoping that the address was still active, she pressed *Send*. The message didn't bounce, fortunately; but with the 12-hour time difference to the other side of the world, she couldn't expect to get an answer until that evening, at the earliest.

Deborah needn't have worried that her message might be overlooked amid a flood of email inquiries. To Dr. Wayan Rawoh, her message arrived — out of the blue — as a kind of vindication, almost a salvation. This was in fact the *first* scholarly communication he had received from outside his own working group.

Prof. Deborah Morrison's message said that she planned to visit Bali, so he immediately sent her instructions about how to contact him, together with a detailed list of things and places she needed to see. And he attached a copy of his full report, *Meteorological Trends for Bali in the Context of Southeast Asia Weather Patterns, 2016-2036.*

Chapter 4

Supersonic flights were just too expensive, so Deborah got herself a seat (more like half a seat, really) on a conventional jumbo jet. This felt different from a normal field trip. For one thing, she had no real plan of research, no outline map that she was working to fill in. Curiosity and anticipation barely allowed her to sleep on the entire 26-hour trip. Emerging, at last, from the airport in Bali, she found a crispness and a fragrance to the air that helped banish her fatigue.

Her plan was to skip the beaches altogether and go straight to Ubud, where she had reserved a room (with her own bathroom, she had made sure) in what they called a "homestay." An arrangement similar to the kinds of places she had often stayed in on her field trips to India.

And she did feel at home, almost as soon as she arrived. Even on the road from the airport, driving an hour or so uphill from the coast, there was plenty to remind her of India. Not only much of the vegetation, but also the exuberant stone carvings of Hindu gods that adorned all the gates and temples along the road. And yet, this place was not quite like anywhere she had been before. There were plenty of people, but not the crowds one saw on the streets of India. And this was the dry season in Bali, without all the dustiness she would have expected.

The sprawling town of Ubud was still known as a cultural and artistic center of Bali — though it had long since been overwhelmed by its own success as a tourist destination. Its main streets reminded Deborah more than anything else of an overpopulated Berkeley: there was a similar concentration of cafes and clothing shops, plus a lot of small Balinese street dogs and minus the proper Berkeley sidewalks. As her taxi slowed, stymied by a good dozen motorcycles, she began to map into her phone some of the places on the list sent by Dr. Rawoh.

Deborah's homestay turned out to be about a quarter of a mile off the main street, up a rutted road that felt much more remote from the town than it actually was. Her host, Ibu Made (MAH-day), was coming out onto the small porch just as her taxi pulled up at the gate.

"Miss Deb-o-rah? Welcome to Ubud!"

Deborah's room was in a modest low building that also housed three other "suites." A young man carried her suitcase onto the stone porch and unlocked the heavy carved wooden door, that creaked open to reveal a canopy bed under a high ceiling. And a stone floor that must feel cool even at midday. (She could not help reflecting, with a hint of self-congratulation, that Jason would have insisted on super AC, as well as the ceiling fan.)

On the other half of the shared front porch, a woman sat reading in a capacious rattan armchair. She immediately looked up from her book.

"Hello there, I'm Candace. Very glad to meet you! I wondered who'd be coming in next." She removed her glasses, conversationally. "I spend part of the year here. Mind you, it's not all that far, coming from Australia. So you can just ask me anything you want to know."

Deborah introduced herself without putting down her shoulder bag. She suddenly felt an overpowering need to be horizontal.

"I'd love to talk some more, after I get on my feet. Long flight from New York."

"Of course, don't mind me at all. You *do* know that the water isn't for drinking, except if it's bottled."

She woke up in the dark. A yellow light shone in through the porch window, from some outdoor fixture — enough for

Deborah to see the room, with its large armoire, and her suitcase standing next to it.

This was Bali!

Just don't drink the water.

Deborah took some time to orient herself, first sitting on the edge of the bed — this was easier than she expected — and then standing on her feet, on the stone floor. *Way* harder. There was a bottle of water in the bathroom, she recalled. But what to do first? Right now, she was dying of thirst *and* desperate to pee. She toddled into the bathroom, grabbed the bottle of water, and sat herself down on the commode.

With this small triumph accomplished, she looked around. The bathroom floor was of stone as well, but rougher, more like paving stones laid directly on the earth. And the far wall of the spacious bathroom was not a wall at all, but a hanging bamboo screen. If you raised the screen (which rolled up), you would be in the garden itself, among the fragrant frangipani and the banana trees that lined the garden wall.

Yes, she would definitely like it here. She drank some more of the water and splashed some on her face.

Checking her phone, Deborah saw it was seven o'clock. PM. Dinner time, then. What she really needed, though, was a cup of coffee. She put on her shoes and went outside to find Ibu Made.

Things began to look up a bit after a tasty dose of caffeine. There were things to do. Unpack her things; shower; get dressed; find some dinner. But first of all, she really had to send a text to Dr. Wayan Rawoh, to inform him that she had arrived in Ubud. She sat down in the rattan porch chair and stared at her phone for a minute, as if she had never seen it before and wasn't sure how it worked.

She had mastered the art of texting just as Candace, coming back from dinner, flowed in through the gate wearing a blue print caftan. Mounting the steps, her energetically pumping elbows put Deborah in mind of a decorative bird of prey.

"I can tell you *just* the place to go for some good local food, a bit up the road that way. Unless you might be craving a pizza, or sushi?"

"Definitely not. But maybe a beer . . . ."

"You can't go wrong with a Bintang, or a Bali Hai. Drinkable and very cheap."

Deborah's phone pinged. Dr. Wayan was welcoming her to Bali. He suggested that they meet for lunch tomorrow, and he sent a map of the proposed location. She showed Candace the map.

"That's not even in Ubud. That place is right out in the country! Should be pretty as a postcard."

Pak Ika is in charge of immigration services at Bali's international airport in Den Pasar. (I should explain that *Pak* is a term of address that literally means "father," but it's used all the time. It's pronounced more or less like PAH. It's respectful without being formal. The corresponding term to address a woman is *Ibu* (EE-boo), meaning "mother.")

Pak Ika (EE-kah) is a government functionary, then. But like many Balinese, he also has a background in the arts: his village had a set of gamelan instruments, and at the age of seven, he was already performing with the group of musicians. Unlike, say, the violin, gamelan is not something you can play — or even practice — on your own. It is an orchestra of at least a dozen types of instrument, mostly made of bronze. Percussive instruments that look something like a xylophone; plus some others like upside-down cooking pots; a couple of drums, and the deeply resonant gongs. Most of the instruments are heavier to carry than a bass fiddle, and none of them plays the full melody. But played together, the rhythmic clinking and clanging and tinkling of these instruments produce dramatic and compelling musical motifs.

Pal Ika's work routine has changed dramatically, ever since he discovered an intriguing app that someone posted on the BasaBali website. It's designed for practicing gamelan. You select your instrument and the piece you want to play, and it plays all the *other* instrument parts, while showing you the notation for your part. (Gamelan notation is written as a series of numbers representing pitch, from 1 to 7.) It's called GamJam, a name Pak Ika considers hideous and undignified. "It should be called Gamelan Karaoke," he has often been heard to mutter.

In any case, when things are slow at the office, Pak Ika likes to open up BasaBali for some gamelan practice, using his computer keyboard to input his part. Today, he plans to play the *ugal*, which allows the player some freedom to add a few stylistic flourishes.

As always, he first scans the BasaBali home page for the news. Immediately, a colorful chart catches his eye: *Meteorological Trends for Bali in the Context of Southeast Asia Weather Patterns, 2016-2036: Temperature*. This chart is unlike anything he has ever seen. A group of colored lines — representing temperature averages for various locations in the Philippines, Malaysia, Thailand, Singapore, and Indonesia — troop across the page, gradually rising, more or less in sync. But the orange line representing Bali follows along with the others only about halfway, and then it *declines*. Pak Ika nods thoughtfully: this chart confirms what he has experienced himself. In fact, he has noticed that in recent years, even the haze of wildfires that covers much of Southeast Asia every dry season seems to avoid the island of Bali. The chart holds the wondering gaze of Pak Ika for several minutes.

Opportunity may perhaps be knocking.

The taxi driver was puzzled. He could get her where she wants to go, no problem. But this was not a place that anyone had ever asked to go to before. "You *sure* that's the place you want to go? There's nothing there!" Farther on, he began to grumble about the state of the road. "Lucky this isn't the rainy season, we would be in mud up to the hubcaps!"

He did manage to find the place, and it was certainly pretty: surrounded by an expanse of rice fields, their mosaic of brilliant green punctuated by lofty coconut palms. And there *was* something there — a modest shop, painted yellow, with some benches in front on which a youngish man was sitting. As the taxi stopped, he stood up and came over.

"You must be Professor Morrison? Welcome to Bali."

Deborah tried to shake hands, awkwardly, while climbing out of the back seat. "Thank you for meeting with me, Dr. Rawoh."

"Please, just call me Wayan."

"And I'm Deborah," she smiled.

A brief conversation ensued between Wayan and the taxi driver. Wayan then turned back to her. "I told him he does not need to wait, as there are a couple of places I want to show you after lunch. I hope that's okay?" He gestured to his motorbike, parked off the road; this was the main mode of transport for most Balinese, including academics.

Jet lag was still framing the question, *Are-you-sure-you-want-to-be-sitting-on-the-back-of-a-bike?* when Deborah's mouth blurted out, "That's great!"

Her brain was now processing paying the taxi driver, but Wayan was already taking care of that too. Then he turned to Deborah and announced, "This is my favorite lunch spot. I want you to meet 'Aunt' Tami, she makes the best fish you'll ever eat." On cue, a small, smiling woman came outside to greet them.

Jet lag surrendered to the occasion. Watching Wayan discuss the lunch with Aunt Tami, Deborah suddenly felt that things were flowing, orderly: everything was going the way things were supposed to go. The language itself seemed to flow around each question, as if capable of handling any problem that might arise.

Wayan struck her as someone who would be equally at home in the rice fields as in the lab. He was maybe five years older than she was, and not much taller, wearing a crisp, brightly patterned short-sleeved shirt with slacks and sandals. Deborah felt overdressed; she would need to buy some lighter weight trousers and some sandals, back in Ubud.

They sat on a bench in the shade of a mango tree, and a young man armed with a machete brought them each a young coconut. He deftly sliced the top off each coconut and then handed them the slices, too, to use as a scoop after drinking the coconut water. This drink was exactly what she wanted, if she had been able to think of it.

Wayan asked about her flight and where she was staying. Had she been to Indonesia before? She explained that her work had been in the subcontinent, mainly in southern India, and that she was excited to see the hints of Indian culture in Bali.

"Yes, India is definitely here," he smiled. "It has been here for about a thousand years. But, as you'll see very soon, we Balinese tend to do things our own way."

Aunt Tami brought out a tray laden with small and large dishes and began to arrange them on the wooden table in front of them. "These are just the side dishes," Wayan explained. There was a plate of glistening greens, that turned out to be deliciously fruity and garlicky; there were finger-sized whole bananas, grilled with coconut; fried and salted red peanuts; mysterious banana-leaf packets; large, puffy chips (introduced as *krupuk*) made of tapioca and dried shrimp; and a small dish of a fiery, bright red salsa called *sambal*. In the center of the table was a large basket of steamed rice. Two warm glasses of tea were set before them. Still to come was the whole grilled fish that (as Wayan told her, proudly) had been pulled from the creek only an hour before, at his direction. When Aunt Tami brought out that fish, Deborah decided that nothing had ever smelled so good.

Deborah's inner clock wasn't sure it it was actually mealtime, but the aromas persuaded her to dig in. Everything was so good, she almost wished she knew how to cook. Wayan apologized as he put down his fork and used his fingers to gather up some rice and fish to pop into his mouth. "Food tastes better, hand to mouth," he insisted. It was unclear to her, though, how that fish could possibly taste any better. As delicate as the freshest trout, but gingery and smoky.

Finally came some plates of fruit — slices of mango, papaya, and meltingly sweet pineapple; and some round, hairy fruits she had not seen in India, called *rambutan*. "The name means that it's hairy – but inside it's just sweet. But with a large stone, be careful." Wayan demonstrated breaking open the red hairy husk to eject the soft white fruit.

Deborah fished out of her bag a couple of the handwash wipes she always traveled with, pleased to be able to make her small contribution to this feast. Wayan was courteously appreciative. They were already thanking Aunt Tami when it occurred to her that Wayan must have taken care of the bill beforehand. He waved away her objections. "You are a guest here, on your first day in Bali." He stood up. "Now, if you are not too tired, I would like to show you a special place where my friends live, not far from here."

Wayan's illustrious guest was younger than he had expected, judging by her position as an Associate Professor of Entomology. And at *Cornell* — an institution long enshrined as the center of American education, as far as Indonesians was concerned. After all, the very first Indonesian-English dictionary had been published there, decades ago.

He was certainly happy to meet Prof. Deborah Morrison, of course, and the lunch had been lively. But hosting a somewhat *older* visitor would perhaps have been more helpful, as a way of demonstrating his own standing as part of an international scientific community.

In any case, for their first site visit, Wayan planned to introduce young Prof. Morrison to the president of Wayan's adopted *banjar*.

It had been a couple of years since Deborah had ridden on the back of a motorbike, in India, under somewhat similar circumstances. She knew to hold on to the seat rather than the driver, and to keep her weight forward. Next time, though, she would have a scarf handy, to keep her hair from whipping her face. But even with her eyes half closed, she was content to drink in the green tones of alternating planted and forested areas as they whizzed by. Flying past the fields and palm trees, and the occasional stone shrine, she felt that this motorbike ride was perhaps worth traveling halfway around the world.

They pulled off the road at a sandy apron in front of an elaborate stone gateway, set into a wall of red brick. Wayan waited as Deborah climbed down, and then he pulled the bike close to the wall before leading the way up some steep steps and through the gate. "This is the banjar I belong to, at least for now, since I live so far from my parents' home."

The walled compound resembled a tiny tropical campus, with several low brick buildings interspersed with trees and flowering shrubs. In the middle Deborah could see a stone stage floor, topped by a thatched roof and shielded by some rattan screens. A couple of children were running around the courtyard, and Wayan called them over. The two stood still, looking abashed as he said a few words to them, and then they ran into the nearest house, on the right of the courtyard.

Wayan explained to Deborah that this was the home of the *banjar* president. "The banjar organizes all the ceremonies for the neighborhood families. Cremations, cleaning the temple — they even show movies. Everyone is involved."

A genial, slightly portly gentleman ambled out of the house, dressed in a tee shirt and a dark sarong. He gave Wayan a wide smile and grabbed his hand. After a brief greeting, Wayan stepped aside to introduce Professor Morrison, in English: "an Associate Professor of Entomology, who has come all the way to Bali, from New York, from Cornell University. She studies rare butterflies."

Handshakes and smiles all around. Wayan said to Deborah, "Pak Nyoman can answer all your questions about how things work in Bali."

Nyoman nodded in acknowledgement, and then turned to Wayan, as they walked into the courtyard. "I haven't seen you since your trip to Malaysia! You must be busy these days."

"Prof. Morrison has read my report, and she thinks it helps explain some of her findings. About butterfly survival."

Nyoman was ushering Deborah and Wayan to some easy chairs of woven rattan, arranged around a low table on his porch. As he took his own seat, he began to talk about the abundance of species in Bali and how they are honored.

"In Bali, we have ceremonies to honor the land and water, as well as our ancestors. Every year there is a ceremony to honor the bats that live in their enormous caves within the mountain, Gunung Agung. The bat cave is a kind of temple, too. We recognize that the bats are carrying the spirit of the earth each night, out into the sky."

For Deborah, who tended to think of bats merely as insect predators, this was a new point of view.

Nyoman's wife emerged and stood in the doorway; she nodded and smiled, but did not join them.

"Foreign visitors," Nyoman continued, "are always surprised to learn that our annual ceremonies happen every 270 days. The Balinese calendar goes by the moon, not the sun. That calendar keeps us all very busy!" He laughed happily at his own joke.

Just then a young woman brought a tray holding cups of tea, and dishes of what looked like small cookies. Wayan took the opportunity to redirect the conversation.

"Prof. Morrison is not here as a tourist. She is researching the status of a specific species of butterfly. Prof. Morrison and her colleagues study butterfly populations all over the world — and it seems that the Balinese climate has created a *unique environment* for butterfly survival."

Nyoman gestured to his guests, inviting them to drink their tea. Wayan ignored his, but Deborah was happy to comply, though she hoped it was okay to take a pass on the cookies.

"While you scientists are analyzing your data, our banjar is taking care of the earth in our own way." Nyoman leaned back with a satisfied grin.

This caught Deborah's attention. "Mr. Nyoman, when are you having your next celebration?"

"It's not a big one. Actually, it is for my own family temple — the cleaning that we do once a year — in a couple of days. But we always do it right!" Another broad grin. "You must come and take photos. But first, let me show you what we're preparing."

Rising bulkily from his chair, Nyoman led the way to the screened pavilion in the center of the courtyard. Pushing one of the screens aside, he waved his hand to indicate a large pile of thin, foot-long long leaves, the color of straw. "This is what we work with: the leaves of the coconut palm." Then, with the flourish of a practiced showman, he pushed open another screen. "This is what we create!"

The center of the pavilion was covered with large and small origami-like decorations, all made of the same straw-like leaves. There were large and small baskets, shaped like boxes or triangles or stars, as well as large weavings that looked like plates or fans, and long clusters of woven fronds. Nyoman pulled out a long, thin bamboo pole. "This is a Balinese Christmas tree. It will stand outside our gate, full of the woven ornaments. We are making four of these poles, two for each side of the gate." He put the pole back. "These will be very simple decorations, of course — not like the ones for the festivals." To Deborah, none of it looked at all simple.

Now Nyoman ushered them through the courtyard to a back corner of the compound. Next to the high brick wall of the compound was an even higher stone shrine, maybe two feet square, topped with a roof made of black thatch (which, Nyoman explained, was used only for the roofs of temples and shrines).

"This is our family temple, to honor all the past generations. We give them thanks for everything we have received from them."

Deborah noticed several small woven baskets, much like the ones piled in the pavilion, that had been placed on a shelf of the shrine. Roughly the size of her hand, each basket held colorful flower petals and a stick of incense.

"Are these for the ceremony next week?" she asked.

Nyoman laughed. "We place an offering here every day, not just once a year. And not only here, but also at every doorway." He turned to point to the nearest door, where three small basket offerings lay on the ground outside, spilling their flower petals. "I told you, we keep ourselves busy!"

Candace was back in the rattan armchair on the porch, apparently absorbed in her book. Deborah was tempted to just sneak past — but she felt it was time to be a bit more sociable.

"I just met the president of a banjar," she announced.

"Ah — the *banjar*! It's a great racket, that is. The families *have* to pay in; and a little gang always runs them, all on their own."

Deborah turned this surprising statement over for a minute. "Can't a family just opt out of joining, if they want to?"

"If nothing else, they've got to have a proper funeral for their parents. The families can't do it on their own. It's always an enormous event, half a dozen or more, all cremated at once, and a big festival. The banjar does all that."

Now Deborah had something more to turn over in her mind. "How does one group have half-a-dozen people all dying at the same time?"

"Well, actually, the family just buries them at first, more or less temporarily. But eventually there's got to be a group cremation, when there are enough families to participate. It's all very impressive — all these gorgeous cremation towers, all made to go up in flames." Candace picked up her book, which had slid off her lap. "They can't just plonk them into the ground and leave them there, the way we do."

Then she had another thought. "Mind you, the banjar is really the thing that kept Bali well out of the 2019 pandemic. The banjars just told their people to stay home, and everyone stayed home. Lots of self-discipline, these Balinese have got." She opened her book, then looked up again.

"Of course, the Balinese have a lot of practice at it anyway — staying inside, I mean. Their biggest holiday is a day when nobody goes out! That's a fact. The whole island turns into a ghost town. It's called *nyepi*. It makes the tourists *so* cross, the ones that weren't expecting it. You really do have to check the calendar for the year, if you don't want to get caught out."

As eager as he was for any and all opportunities to present his life's work, Wayan was not quite ready to bring Deborah to see the terraced fields of rice, and their intricate irrigation canals. In his experience, newly arrived foreigners often didn't have eyes for what was most important. He came up with a better plan: today, they would visit a place that tells the larger story — a place that had kept its mysteries, but that spoke clearly enough just the same. They would visit the nearby temple in a cave: the "Elephant Cave," *Goa Gajah*.

In fact, the site had nothing at all to do with actual elephants (animals which had never roamed the island of Bali, in any case). It was a shrine dedicated to Ganesha, the Hindu god of wisdom, who is always represented as having the head of an elephant. A statue of Ganesha was located inside the cave, serving as an ancient focus of meditation, and an equally ancient Hindu temple stood nearby, outside the cave.

Wayan texted Deborah: *I pick you up tomorrow @ 9 okay?*

Chapter 5

At 9:00 am, Deborah was ready to launch, having been at least half awake since 5:00 am. She found she was actually looking forward to the motorbike ride, as a great way to wake up with zero effort on her part.

Twenty minutes later, they arrived at the Elephant Cave. Or rather, at its huge parking area, ringed with an assortment of souvenir stalls and food stands. Wayan parked the motorbike in the designated area and led the way to the site entrance. Deborah was glad she had worn her running shoes for navigating the long stone stairway that led from the parking lot down to the large temple courtyard.

Here, instead of tourist shops, she saw an array of temples and pavilions, with their distinctive thatched roofs, and a series of impressive stone statues. The cave itself could be glimpsed in the far corner, announced by a stone entrance exuberantly embellished with carvings of other-worldly demons and gargoyles.

Deborah insisted on buying their tickets at the kiosk, over Wayan's objections (hoping that this did not cause him any loss of face). Wayan in turn took charge of renting the traditional sarong and sash for each of them to wear — an obligatory sign of respect for the sacred site. Deborah smiled as she wrapped herself in this brightly colored ensemble, so out of place with her khaki field shirt.

The courtyard was far more inviting than the commercial and touristy parking lot above. A few selfies were going on, though there were not very many tourists at this hour. They stopped at the large, central bathing pool. Half a dozen people in sarongs were standing in the waist-deep water, reached by a short flight of stone steps. Six tall stone statues, carved in the Indian style, were ranged alongside the pool: six imposing female figures, each pouring a constant flow of water out of a stone jug. For the Balinese, Wayan explained, this pool is a site of purification. People who come to bathe in the pool immerse themselves and pray at each of the statues, which represent six sacred rivers of India. This cleansing is a preparation for meditation in the cave itself.

They wordlessly agree to bypass the bathing ritual and go on to the cave. There is something eerie about entering a cave, and this one seemed especially intimidating, beneath the monstrous, ogre-ish face that dominated the carved façade. Wayan explained that the giant mouth of the demon repesents *time* — a creature that no one and nothing can avoid. This giant, called Kala, serves to keep bad spirits away from the cave and to protect the devotees meditating inside.

The smell of incense met them at the threshold of the cave, and inside, the incense mixed with the smell of the earth itself. As her eyes adjusted to the darkness, Deborah could see the main object of devotion: a somehow cheerful-looking stone elephant, crowned with what looked like a stone wig, sitting on its stone pedestal in a cross-legged posture of meditation. There were a couple of people sitting on the ground, holding incense sticks, evidently in meditation or prayer. Wayan quietly pointed out the niches in the cave walls where priests once sat to meditate. After a few minutes, Deborah feels quite ready to go back into the sunshine.

Outside, the extensive grounds of the temple invited exploration. They followed a winding path down a forested hillside, crossing a stream on a stone bridge. Palm trees and mango trees reached high into the sky, partly shrouded by a netting of vines and aerial roots reaching to the ground. Lotus ponds invited tourists to linger.

Wayan pointed out a huge banyan tree — considered sacred by the Balinese. The banyan sends roots down into the ground from its branches, and over time the maze of roots from a single tree begins to resemble a small forest. As they reached its shelter, he turned to look at the gurgling stream nearby.

"Two streams come together on this site," he told her. "Up above, the streams create a steady flow of water into the bathing pool. I imagine that this is why this spot was chosen to build a temple, perhaps even more than because of the cave."

They turned and made their way back up the path to the courtyard, and then up the long stairs to the parking area.

"Maybe there will be someone up there selling those wonderful coconuts," Deborah wished out loud — feeling more than a little parched and tired, on her second full day in Bali. And, yes! As if answering her wish, there was a young man standing next to a heap of husked coconuts, just begging to be sliced open.

They found a patch of level ground in the shade of a nearby tree, content to sit for a while and drink their coconuts. Quietly, with his eyes on the distant hill, Wayan began to share his own feeling about this sacred place.

"This is the same water that gives life to the rice fields, and to Bali," he said. "The Balinese religion is called *agama tirta*, the 'religion of holy water.' But *we* don't make the water holy; even the priests don't make the water holy." He held his now-empty coconut in both hands. "We believe that water is holy because it comes from nature, because it keeps everything alive." He paused and grew thoughtful, as if seeking wisdom from the coconut. Deborah remained quiet, sensing that he had something more to say.

"There is nothing at all sacred about the research I do," he continued. "But I'm beginning to think that the questions it raises seem to touch on sacred mysteries, the secrets of the earth and water. *Of course* scientists don't want to go there. . . ." He suddenly stopped himself, embarrassed. "Don't mind me, Deborah. We Balinese tend to see spirits everywhere!"

Now Deborah felt embarrassed. She felt as if she, personally, carried with her the entire baggage of Western materialism. But if that was her designated role, this was her cue. She put her coconut to one side.

"You are forgetting, Wayan," she said gently, "I have read your report. I do *not* think that you are seeing spirits." He looked at her questioningly.

"It's clear that you have examined every possible scientific explanation: ocean currents, equatorial phenomena, even the magnetic polar shift. And the monitoring system you use was rechecked, and duplicated. That's not my idea of somebody going all mystic! That is how people do science."

Wayan's face, even his body, relaxed into a smile. His steady gaze rested on her face for a full minute. "Thank you for being such a careful reader, Deborah."

Oh, good lord! Was she actually *blushing*? Deborah began to study her own hands, embarrassed now on a whole new level.

But her brain could still function, and she was beginning to see a clearer picture. It seemed that Wayan's stunning climate findings must be getting little or no attention in his professional circles. There could be lots of explanations for that, of course — including that ever-present wild card, professional jealousy. But she could easily imagine a bigger reason: a generalized hyper-sensitivity, among scientists, to anything that might suggest the work of a *climate contrarian*. Only two decades ago, climate science had been plagued with claims of contrary findings, based on some slim and overly selective "research."

As if following Deborah's musings, Wayan picked up the thread again. "I think my colleagues might have been more interested if I had left a few stones unturned, if I had left open a few explanations for them to explore. Or, maybe, if I could have presented a proper hypothesis." He leaned back against the tree, looking up through its branches. "Maybe it was premature for me to present the findings in Kuala Lumpur, without having an explanatory framework."

You can't get a buzz from drinking coconut water, even fresh from the tree, so it must have been the combination of jet lag and fatigue. No longer the scientist, Deborah spoke almost without thinking.

"Maybe," she murmured, looking at Wayan and shrugging her shoulders, "maybe these caves and streams will turn out to be your framework."

Still looking at the sky, Wayan slightly nodded. They sat for a minute or two without talking, hearing, amid the silence, water flowing somewhere in the background. And then, with no apparent signal, they got to their feet to walk back to the motorbike corral.

Getting back on the bike felt surprisingly comfortable to Deborah. They were almost back in Ubud when she described, to herself, this comfortable feeling. The word she found was *trust*.

By the time they arrived at her homestay, Deborah's inner clock had started campaigning for a nap; but she was determined to make better use of the daylight. Saying goodbye to Wayan, she announced (in part to convince herself), "I think I'll get some lunch in town and do some shopping."

"Excellent idea. And don't forget," Wayan said over his shoulder, as he turned his bike back onto the road, "tomorrow will be the family ceremony at Pak Nyoman's house. We can visit some rice fields the next day."

As she closed the gate behind her, Deborah found herself wondering whether this was maybe some kind of dating. In any case, it seemed clear that Wayan was perfectly happy to spend his time hosting her. Not for the first time, she wished she had some of Cecily's "girly smarts." Heck, she didn't even know whether *she* was interested in *him*, let alone whether *he* was interested in *her.*

But Bali was turning out to be enormously interesting, and Deborah couldn't wait to get a look at the photos she had taken at the Elephant Cave. For the first time in maybe twenty years, she actually had the urge to make some sketches: of the banyan tree maybe, and the pool with its statues, and the elaborately carved entrance to the cave itself. Shopping, she decided, must include buying herself a sketchbook and some pencils.

Candace, sitting at a patio table, looked up from her lunch of fresh fruit.

"Now, what have you seen so far?" she asked.

Yes, she knew the Elephant Cave very well. Such an impressive ancient site, "old as the hills."

"And did you see the 8th century Buddhist statues? That whole place is simply amazing — all Hindu on the one side, and all really old Buddhist on the other." She cut open her mangosteen, a hard, brown, unpromising-looking (but delicious) piece of fruit. "But you haven't yet seen any of the dances. There's a Barong dance this evening at the Ubud Palace, well worth seeing. It's very mystical. The Barong is a lovely, fluffy great lion, a bit like a Chinese dragon . . ."

Deborah quickly thanked her for the suggestion, even though she suddenly wanted to scream, "I AM NOT HERE AS A TOURIST!!!" Instead, she calmly asked Candace for some suggestions of places to buy some sandals and wearable clothing.

"There's a couple of places." Candace reached for a scrap of paper and her pen. "You're going to that family ceremony tomorrow, right? You'll want a pair of flip-flops for going visiting, then — easy to slip off at the doorstep. The way they all do here."

Wayan picked her up mid-morning, to go to Nyoman's "small" family celebration. The family would have performed their private ceremonies early in the morning, he explained, by placing special offerings at the family shrine. You couldn't miss the gate — now gracefully framed by four towering, lavishly decorated bamboo poles. A small crowd of people was spilling into the street.

"It looks like the whole neighborhood showed up," Deborah observed.

"It would be disrespectful to stay away," Wayan answered. "Besides, everyone knows there will be food!"

Wayan led the way up the stone steps to the narrow gate of the compound, where they stood for a minute overlooking the jostling and laughing crowd in the courtyard. Deborah's mind went back to her experiences of celebrations in India; but this seemed different. The smells were different — an unfamiliar palette of spices; and the language flowing around her seemed to have its own music, a mix of smooth and staccato tones. And she did not see a clearly discernible women's area, but only undifferentiated clusters of guests.

It wasn't hard to identify their host, who was laughing and gesturing in the middle of a knot of people. Wayan pointed out the shrine by the back wall, which had been laden with offerings and wrapped in a black-and-white checked cloth. "That cloth is the Balinese yin and yang," he explained. "Good and evil are never completely separated."

Indeed, there was food being served. Deborah could see two or three young men making their way through the crowd, each carrying a huge platter of rice or grilled meat. Guests sat to eat on every convenient step or wall, and even along the edge of the central pavilion, which had been transformed into a performance stage.

The pavilion, she saw, had been carpeted and hung with decorations; the rattan screens had been moved to the back, forming a backdrop. And sitting on the stage were maybe a dozen musicians, wearing black tee shirts and gilded head wraps: all of them men, of varying ages. Each of them was sitting on the floor behind an impressive instrument, wielding a kind of mallet to strike notes with amazing rapidity. Most of the instruments looked like a cross between a brass xylophone and a camp stove; some looked like a set of upside-down brass bowls, arrayed in an elaborately carved wooden frame. Several huge gongs were hanging at the back of the group, almost hiding from view the gong player. And in the front sat a man who seemed to be the director, playing a double-faced drum that he held in his lap.

As Wayan turned to lead the way down the steps and into the crowd, Deborah motioned to him to wait. Standing there on the steps, she had the best view of the stage and the players. This was music (she felt) that demanded attention. It was loud and percussive — ringing, reverberating music that seemed to celebrate its own energy. But there was something else about it, something that Deborah found hauntingly familiar. Somewhere, beneath the layers of chiming notes, she was hearing the sound of a forest at night, recalling the incessant thrum of the orchestra of insects. Its effect on her was transfixing, creating a sense of expectation. Those rollicking sounds of celebration contained a questioning note, an undertone of uncertainty, as if this enchanting music embraced the world in all its complexity.

The musicians were about to conclude the piece they were playing. The notes became more leisurely, more widely spaced, and then suddenly speeded up again, racing to an abrupt finish. Deborah looked around, wondering whether any of the guests — who were mostly talking or eating, or both — had been listening to the music at all.

Wayan looked back at Deborah; she nodded that she was ready to follow his lead and dive into the crowded courtyard. Nyoman spotted them immediately.

"Thank you for coming, Professor!" Nyoman greeted them, arms wide, and then turned and gestured to a couple of young people standing next to him. "This is my son, Dik, and my daughter, Dina. The Professor has come all the way from New York to help us celebrate!"

There was general laughter, followed by a round of handshakes. Deborah found herself gently but firmly steered to a nearby table, covered with a plastic cloth, that was instantly abandoned by its previous occupants. After seating them both, Nyoman gave some instructions to Dina and then joined them at the table. Someone placed a water bottle before each of them — kind of a third-world throwback, she decided.

"So, Madam Professor, what do you think of our gamelan music? Is this the first time you have heard the gamelan?" As a dutiful host, he had no doubt noticed her paying rapt attention to the music.

Deborah gave an enthusiastic nod, as she took a long drink from the water bottle. "I've never heard anything like it before. It's like music from another planet!"

Nyoman was obviously pleased with this response, and he tossed off an order of some kind to someone standing behind him. The gamelan players began to play another piece.

"I had this set of instruments made specially, just a few years ago. In honor of my parents. We brought them here from Den Pasar. The gamelan maker brought them here personally, so he could tune them again — here, in their new home. It took him a week to tune them all."

"Do you play it also?"

Nyoman laughed. "I used to play with a neighborhood group. But now I let other people do it. My legs are too stiff to sit on the floor for so long!"

Trays of food arrived and absorbed everyone's attention. Nyoman began to serve his special guests all the choicest portions, unheeding Deborah's protests. As they began to eat, he excused himself to see to some new arrivals. Deborah noticed that, like many of the guests, Wayan ate using his fingers rather than a fork.

"There are always some guests who come to eat the food," Wayan commented, "and then you hear them complain."

"About the food?"

"No, about the money. They don't want to pay dues for the banjar — but they're happy to attend all the events."

"Why don't they just leave the banjar?"

Wayan explained, much as Candace had, that every family will need the help of the banjar for their own ceremonies. "And we really don't have anything to complain about. The money does get spent on the events, not like some other banjars."

Deborah could see people still coming into the gate, as other people were leaving. She wondered out loud, "When is the party over?"

Wayan laughed. "Some folks will stay all night!"

Riding home, Wayan's mind kept returning to the image of Deborah standing still at the courtyard entrance, clearly awestruck, listening intently to the gamelan. This was the music he had heard for his entire life, and it made a powerful impression on him, to see someone else hearing it for the first time.

Deborah was glad to get back to her room without having to talk with anyone. She had found the festivities surprisingly enjoyable, considering that she did not know the language being spoken. Even now, she was hearing the gamelan music in her head. She was still mystified by its power, its ability to sweep her up inside it — this music that echoes mysterious portents, even in the midst of celebration.

How different this trip was, from her other research trips! Well, to be honest, she wasn't actually doing any research at all — but in just three short days, she already felt part of her surroundings, more than on any other trip. Maybe more than she would feel on her home ground, in upstate New York. And maybe she should begin to face the obvious fact, that this sense of home had a lot to do with seeing Wayan.

Chapter 6

The next morning, on the way to visit the rice farms, Deborah asked if they could stop and get a cup of coffee. After passing right by a few nice-looking cafes, they finally stopped at a place that had no sign and no parking. "This is the best coffee in Ubud," Wayan assured her. "And they make the best fried bananas too."

As they sipped their excellent coffees, Wayan had a confession. He had been especially pleased to have a visitor to show around, partly because he needed an excuse to take a break from work. He felt he needed to clear his head of the day-to-day details, to think about a strategy for publishing his data. He could let his assistant take care of recording the measurements for a few days.

"But the truth is, your visit is also helping me see a bigger picture, see the landscape with new eyes. So, I feel very grateful," he said (speaking, now, almost formally), "for the privilege of hosting you this week."

Okay, Deborah thought, I guess he's not actually *interested*. Feeling, stupidly, a bit let down, she quickly assured him that she had very much enjoyed seeing the sights.

"But," she could not help pointing out, "I'm really not here as a tourist!"

Wayan answered, smiling, "Neither am I." He looked thoughtful. "Bali is the same, whether for tourists or scholars. It's only the eyes that differ." His eyes met hers.

"I have to thank you for something else as well," he said. "In Kuala Lumpur, I realized that no one is going to take my research seriously unless it is published in a scientific journal. I suddenly realized that my findings could sound like the work of a *climate denier* — of all things! It has been a relief to me to be able to share my research with you."

Deborah nodded and managed a smile.

They were finishing their coffees when Wayan seemed to have a new thought. "I want to ask you something, Deborah, if you don't mind."

"Of course!"

"You seemed to really enjoy listening to the gamelan, at Pak Nyoman's."

"Mmm, yes. I really loved hearing that music."

"Is it possible for you to tell me how it sounded to you, hearing the gamelan for the first time?"

Deborah had to think for a moment. "For me, it sounded as if there were different layers in the music. Different layers with their own meanings, maybe? I thought I was hearing a kind of background tone, through the whole piece, that seemed to create a feeling of mystery."

Wayan nodded, listening carefully.

"Later, I was thinking that Western music works differently. You might hear some music that sounds haunting, from another world, but then the piece can change its tone completely. The only example I could think of is our classic Wedding March — it begins with a few notes that sound almost ominous, and then it launches right away into this big celebration."

Once again Deborah felt a blush coming on. Had she really, actually, turned the topic to *weddings*???

"Anyway," she hurried on, "in the gamelan piece, it seems very different. Those mysterious tones seem to be mixed up in the celebration, too."

Wayan nodded again. "I think that the mysterious tone you are hearing may be the *offering* — the prayer that is always part of our music."

Maybe her eyes really had begun to see differently. Visiting the rice fields that day felt very different from touring the Elephant Cave. The geometric quilt of the diked rice fields illustrated the plant's stages of growth and ripening, through subtle shifts of color from light green to dark green and then to ripe yellow. In one of the fields four women were bending to work, under their straw hats, laboriously transplanting the young shoots of rice into the flooded field. Farther in the distance, a row of flooded fields glittered in the sun, as if framing the entire scene. The constellation of rice paddies charmed Deborah like nothing else she had seen in Bali.

On aesthetic grounds alone, this scene would rank as a world heritage treasure. But for Wayan, the miracle of engineering was the real treasure. A thousand years ago (he explained), while people elsewhere in the world were laboring, presumably under duress, to construct monumental temples and tombs (looking at you, Java and Mexico and Egypt!), the ancient Balinese were developing a system for *sharing water*, to ensure fair access throughout their mountainous land. Water was carefully channeled, from the wide trenches dug along the upper fields, through ever-narrower ditches farther downhill. The fields themselves were leveled, creating those famously picturesque terraces with shimmering water protecting the delicate, pale green shoots of newly transplanted rice. Once the plants are established — taller, and bright green — that field can be drained, and the water will be sent to some other field that has been made ready for transplanting.

Like the original builders of these trenches and dikes, Balinese farmers work constantly and meticulously to maintain the barriers that channel the water. And most impressively, each season they have to reach an agreement, together, on the precise timing for releasing the water to the neighboring downhill fields.

That's why (Wayan explained) there was also a bureaucratic system for deciding on water access, a system that was possibly as old as the channels and dikes themselves. Each district in Bali has a water official who is elected by the member households, and who has final say on the timing of water release. But since he has no power of enforcement, he has to work closely with the farmers each season.

Wayan pointed out the small, elevated shrine in the corner of a field. "This shrine marks ownership of the farm," he explained. "But it also shows that managing the land and the water is a central part of our religion. We call it the religion of water — *agama tirta.*"

They walked farther along the earthen dike, in single file.

"Having an argument over water would be the *opposite* of placing a blessing on the earth," he mused. "The rice fields give me the same feeling as at the Elephant Cave. Sacred water and sacred earth are always connected: earth and water are a whole."

The sun was beginning to set, promptly around 6 pm (as always on the equator). They retraced their steps along the narrow grassy ridges bordering the canals. Here and there were clumps of manioc, and Wayan pointed out the fish living in the ditches and ducks parading through fields, providing natural sources of fertilizer as well as food. Balinese farmers had discontinued the overuse of chemical pesticides and fertilizers decades ago, precisely so that their fields could sustain a healthy biodiversity.

And then, finally, there it was, fluttering around a manioc plant. *Ideopsis juventa juventa,* going about its butterfly business — no doubt unaware of this stranger who had traveled halfway around the globe to take its picture. Deborah immediately got some burst-action shots, before her brain had a chance to get all congratulatory. The butterfly circled and landed on a plant closer to her and began slowly fanning its black-and-white, art deco, leaded-glass wings.

That evening, in her hotel room, Deborah dictated a summary record of the location and timing of the sighting — which was also recorded automatically on the photos she uploaded — together with a description of its immediate environment. It suddenly struck her how extraordinary it had felt, to spend a day walking for several miles amid green and growing, unstressed plant life, under healthy-looking trees. This experience was a real-life demonstration of Wayan's weather chart: Bali's climate seemed to be completely unaffected by the ravages of heat, floods, and drought.

And something else struck her, as well. As excited as she was to see her butterfly — *maybe that was not even the best part of the day*.

Humming, Deborah quickly triple-saved the photos and video of her Wood Nymph. Now, she sent the most decorative photo and a short video in a text message to Cecily, with an exuberant caption: #**bali**okay.

And: when Cecily posts that video — along with the #**bali**okay hashtag — the thing will go viral.

Novels get it all wrong, Deborah thought. Okay, here she was lying in her bed and thinking about someone she had met. But it wasn't anything about how he *looked* — tall or short, blond or dark. Or, even, about how he looked at *her*.

It was simply that feeling of trust: something she could sense by looking at his face, or seeing the way he moved, or just sensing him in the same room. And, especially, his voice.

Deborah had never spent a lot of time on social media, but now she began to track #**bali**okay. One of the posts came as a rather charming surprise: a photo that had nothing to do with green landscapes or pretty butterflies. It was the image of a simple, small woven basket holding a few marigold flowers, set on a patch of cut grass.

Deborah recognized the image immediately. It was the traditional daily offering that is placed on every family temple. Or rather, this was the offering that is placed *on the ground,* at each home, shop, or ricefield. She immediately forwarded the post to Wayan.

Wayan had a habit of ignoring his phone for hours — sometimes even days at a time. Since Deborah's arrival, however, he had developed a new habit: almost like a teen-ager (he chided himself), he checked his phone regularly, whenever they were not together. So, he immediately saw the forwarded image of the earth offering. He stared at the image for a full minute, as if it carried an actual message, intended personally for him. He was seeing all over again those two offering baskets from his dream in that Kuala Lumpur hotel room, the two sacred offerings that dissolved into air. He couldn't shake the feeling that there was a message here, something significant.

When he met Deborah the next day, Wayan asked her if she knew the person who sent that photo. Together they googled the name: Teresa Campbell was an anthropologist living in Bali.

Chapter 7

A single sighting, of course, did not amount to *data*. However thrilled the internet may have been with that video, Deborah still needed to develop a map of field results, positive and negative. She reached out to Stefan, in case he had some suggestions of promising locales, but all he could come up with were the same broad guidelines that she had followed for the past eight years. Find a range of contrasting environments (he advised), preferably demonstrating some quantifiable variables (temperature, air and ground moisture, percentage of unbuilt area, etc.). Right.

Fortunately, Wayan was able to provide more specific guidance. Together they developed a map of some promising and not-so-promising areas to be explored — some of them forested, some farmed, some built up. Deborah had planned to engage a driver by the day to take her back and forth, but Wayan insisted on being part of the mission of butterfly discovery. In any case, he assured her, she would be better off on the motorcycle for navigating the pathways outside of town.

Deborah had been in Bali for only a week, but she was already feeling the familiar pings of research anxiety, feeling already behind schedule and under-equipped. That feeling made no sense, of course. She had everything that she always used to document a site visit: time-and-GPS-stamped voice memos, photos, and videos, as well as scene-capture "aureos." Whether or not there were actual sightings, all this documentation would provide valuable data. But though she fully believed her own pep talk, Deborah couldn't quite shake off the research "butterflies."

It felt reassuring to have Wayan's company for this first field research trip, and on the back of his motorbike she had almost a 360-degree view of the landscape they were passing. Wayan seemed eager to share bits of local history and cultural lore, shouting over the engine noise, as they drove farther from the tourist-ridden and motorcycle-clogged streets of Ubud. He even had a good sense of likely habitats: the second place they stopped was not actually on their list, but it offered some promising areas to explore. To tell the truth, this was Deborah's own preferred habitat, a second-growth forest that provided canopy but also sunlight, for flowering ground vegetation.

Her mind and instincts switched into tracking mode, focused on carefully creating a semi-continuous site record. But now, she began to wish she had come with only a driver. Honestly, all the extraneous information was not what she needed right now — details about the landscape and its previous condition, or about local beliefs. This was the first time, in her eight years of research, that she had experienced *conversation* at a field site.

But the butterflies apparently didn't mind people talking. Among several attractive dark blue and iridescent species (whose food plants, she knew, were not in the milkweed family), there were, indeed, two delicate black-and-white Wood Nymphs.

Deborah marked this unexpected forest site for a follow-up trip, double-checking that all her records were saved. She was anxious to get to all the other nearby sites on her list before the light began to fade. Walking back to the motorbike, she noticed an abandoned-looking shrine, a couple of yards off their path. Feeling more conversational now, she asked Wayan whether that shrine would have once marked the corner of someone's rice field. Wayan turned to look at it, and he stopped walking. The shrine was unusually high — a thin column almost like a pencil, and it leaned a bit toward them.

For a long moment, Wayan had nothing to say, standing still and seeming to look past the shrine into the little forest. All he said, when they started walking again, was: "Dr. Deborah, you must now talk to Teresa Campbell."

What had happened to her? She must have been possessed. Of course, she was tired by then, still a bit jet-lagged and getting hungry for some dinner. None of this was an excuse.

What Deborah said to Wayan, at that moment, was this:

"Wayan, I thought you were a *scientist.*"

The words were still in her ears when she realized how horrible this must sound, to someone whose life's work had gotten so little respect. And what did she even *mean* by that? This Teresa was an anthropologist, after all. Isn't that a kind of science too? Deborah's father, a geologist, had told her often enough that science was a *method*, not a fraternity. Who was she to be telling Wayan what was and was not scientific information? Or, maybe, that his own treasure trove of information about Balinese practices and beliefs could be of no interest to a *real scientist.* She gagged on her own wayward tongue.

The motorbike ride to the next site was spent in silence. Deborah had apologized on the spot, as best she could, painfully aware that the words could not be explained away. She spent those 10 kilometers in thought. How could she make proper amends to Wayan? More important, what was going on with her own notion of "science"? Fieldwork was her comfort zone, she realized: documenting specimens and locations. But her data was all about the *what.* None of the tools she used would be of any use in figuring out the *why.* If, somehow, she found no signs of stress for *Ideopsis juventa juventa* in Bali, what exactly were the factors to help explain the anomaly? Would those factors turn out to be the same as the factors underlying Wayan's completely unbelievable weather findings? In any case, why on earth would she throw away the chance to learn about, and perhaps build on, Wayan's understanding of this strange dynamic?

Deborah had not felt this ashamed since the time she let the air out of her big sister's bicycle tires.

They dismounted at the next field site. Wayan began to lead the way, but Deborah hesitated. "I'm so sorry, Dr. Wayan. I really need to say something to you." He turned back, wearing his normal friendly smile. Deborah wondered if he could even mean it.

"Honestly," she blurted out, "I wouldn't blame you if you dropped this project completely." She looked at the ground, avoiding his gaze. "I'm really not as stupid as I sounded back there. I do want to do serious science — and *of course* a serious scientist needs to talk to the experts." She looked up at him. "My butterflies are not going to tell me what's going on."

Wayan laughed in agreement.

"Dr. Wayan," she announced formally, "I hope you will help me find Teresa Campbell."

The sun was setting as they rode back to Ubud. They again rode silently, each of them breathing in the pink and coral light of the sky, magically reflected in the flooded rice fields. When they got to Deborah's hotel, she invited Wayan to join her for dinner, but he made an excuse.

"Tomorrow night then. Or Wednesday? I insist." It was the very least she could do, by way of a thank-you.

"Ya got to be fucking kidding. It's impossible. A six-year project using artificial intelligence — combining satellite data on global temperature and rainfall, even weather events. You crunch those numbers, spit out the results. *And you get the same result as if you just looked at Instagram!*" Godfrey Kline's assistant knew better than to interrupt the boss. "Okay, I know. It's about crowdsourcing, the intelligence of crowds. It's *supposed* to work, we do it too. But *Instagram*??"

"Actually, sir, it's called Pict these days."

"I don't care if it's called toilet paper. I want to know where the data is coming from. Who was it that shared this 'Bali OK' stuff? Originally?"

The U.S. has had a Climate Czar for several years. Godfrey Kline's job is to restore and reconstitute the research capability that was lost when the "fossils" were in charge. Most days, the job makes him a bit grouchy. Especially when it starts to look pointless.

One of their research tools is a crowdsourcing platform, based on mobile phone data. Mobile tech has achieved saturation levels all over the world, and now they can get real-time information about environmental issues of all kinds, in just about every part of the globe. And not only is the data crowdsourced; the solutions are too, potentially. There's a small global army of interested (and, to some extent, panicked) subscribers to this data, who have signed on to try to ameliorate the issues as soon as they get reported from the field. This global group of volunteers has developed a clearinghouse of resources, available to be matched with the problems.

That was the original idea, anyway, but the *action* side has tended to be limited. The reports keep coming in — and the system is getting overwhelmed. There are no longer isolated areas of disaster. There is just disaster.

Except: the data analytics show that there's one area, just a couple thousand square miles, in the middle of Indonesia, that has not been pinging any climate alerts. South of Borneo and east of Java. An island, literally as well as metaphorically. In fact, the Czar's massive database of climate reporting has come up with the same results that have been illustrated so clearly in photos posted on Pict and Gram — those bright green ricefields, the mountain slopes covered in deep tropical forest. The same results conveyed by that idiotic hashtag, #**bali**okay.

And *only* in Bali. Not Thailand, not Malaysia or the Philippines or Fiji. Though of course, there isn't really a Fiji any more; the Fijians have been forced to join in the worldwide exodus from various unliveable lands.

Wayan did accept her invitation to dinner. With input from Candace and Ibu Made, Deborah had selected an upscale Balinese-style restaurant, built in a series of small wooden pavilions over and around a small stream.

"The food is wonderful, and you do get absolute privacy. There are even bamboo shades you can lower down." Candace had a knowing smirk — as if there were something to "know."

Maybe it was actually the sense of privacy, in their semi-curtained pavilion, that made it difficult to talk. Why was it easier to have a conversation by yelling over the noise of the motorbike? Her reticence made her cross with herself, which didn't help matters. Why should this even be awkward? They were professional colleagues discussing a project, after all — *not* a couple on a date. If Bali were Moslem, you might expect to find some constraints on talking or eating with the opposite sex. But Bali's Hindu-Buddhist tradition seemed quite relaxed in that regard, from everything she could see of daily life.

"Deborah," she told herself, "it's time to relax." She took a yoga breath, and another one, and then turned her attention to the skewered shrimp appetizer. She squeezed a lime over the dish and offered it to Wayan, who (of course) politely offered it right back. Biting a tender shrimp from its skewer, Deborah *mmm'd* her appreciation: there was certainly garlic there, and the bite from a chili, and some other flavor she didn't recognize. Wayan polished off a skewer and nodded his approval. He complimented the waiter, who had returned bringing the next dish. And then began to ask him what he knew about the stream that ran through the property. Where was its source, and how much did it vary seasonally? Ah, Deborah thought, this *was* the perfect spot to bring an irrigation expert!

Only half-listening to their water conversation, Deborah continued to coach herself. You *do* know how to "think-not-think," she reminded herself. First, figure out what the question is; and then, completely let it go, like a butterfly that cannot be corralled. It's like letting your eyes rest at the end of the day, just before you go to sleep. So, deliberately relaxing her eyes, she began to see the restaurant laid out as a map. There was the stream, and half a dozen pavilions, and the small building that housed the kitchen, with saronged waiters coming and going.

How out of place would she feel, she wondered suddenly, if she were to walk into that kitchen? The kitchen, of course, would be where people were speaking Balinese. No doubt it would have its own little shrine, with daily offerings of flowers. The kitchen was part of Bali. But was their dining pavilion even in Bali at all? Was that how Wayan was experiencing this elegant dinner over a stream?

As delicious as the food was, this dinner began to seem like a lame idea for a thank-you. Of course, if Deborah had a home here, she could have hosted a friendly dinner of her own.

Instead, she had to take Wayan away from Bali, to this nobody's-land.

Deborah would definitely need a more sophisticated way to reciprocate all the patient help Wayan had offered her. She needed to become a better learner.

"Let's figure out how we're going to meet Teresa Campbell. I can send a message back to her and invite her to lunch. How about Friday?"

That night, while trying to fall asleep, Deborah found herself chasing a bunch of mental rabbits. How did everything get so complicated? This was a research trip, and she knew how to do research. On these trips, you always needed to find people who could help steer you through unfamiliar situations — the inevitable bureaucratic hurdles and logistic problems. And you always found appropriate ways to show appreciation for all their help. Like, treating them to an excellent restaurant dinner. Well done, Deb, she told herself.

Which led to a different rabbit. Why did she need to give herself *lectures* at all? Why not just enjoy a good dinner and get on with the project?

And now, here came the most annoying rabbit of all, the one she somehow couldn't shake. Was this what had happened with Jason, her inability to let simple things be simple? Or did things get complicated because *he* made them that way?

Maybe his habit of near-constant fault-finding had trained her too well, to find fault with almost everything she did.

The morning brought glorious sunshine, and with it a better mood. Of course she wanted things to go smoothly with Wayan, who had been so generous not only with logistic help but also with his insights. She was more or less in the position of a student, who still had much to learn. So, she sent him a text to announce her new plan for the day. She would postpone her next field visit and, instead, visit nearby Bali Park. Trying to learn about Balinese traditions (she had lectured herself) did not make her a tourist.

Indeed, Bali Park was a popular tourist attraction, half an hour outside Ubud. It was a nicely landscaped park covering several acres, all laid out in intersecting paths, designed to showcase specimens of Balinese culture: stone carving, painting, dance costumes and masks, textiles, ceremonial decorations, and offerings. It was a place to encounter Balinese houses and temples, not in their natural setting, but presented with explanatory plaques in several languages. Like an outdoor museum.

Wayan texted back: *Never been to BP, I'll join you*.

It felt a bit like having the professor join your study group, just as you were breaking out the Cliff Notes.

Even with Wayan accompanying her, Deborah kept to her original plan, to hire (for a modest fee) a park guide. He was a tall, polite young man with excellent English. He greeted Wayan in Balinese; Wayan answered in English, and followed up with a technical question — to eliminate any possible confusion about their relative status.

Their first stop was a replica of a family compound, very similar to Nyoman's, with its high brick wall and the narrow gate, reached by a steep flight of stone steps. The wall enclosed a courtyard, with a central pavilion surrounded by four or five separate living quarters. The guide pointed out the outdoor cooking area at the back, and the family shrine roofed with black thatch.

"The shrine is always located in the northeast corner," he told them.

The next site was a replica of a village temple, also set in a courtyard surrounded by a high brick wall, and also reached by steep steps and a narrow stone gate. Deborah remarked to Wayan that none of these places were designed to be accessible, say, if you were in a wheelchair.

"Very true," he agreed solemnly, "because they are designed to be inaccessible to evil spirits, who cannot climb stairs or fit through narrow spaces."

The temple itself was basically an elaborate stone carving, with a long flight of stone steps in front. The guide explained that you don't go inside the structure, as you would a church; it actually has no "inside." Ceremonies would take place in the temple courtyard, and offerings would be placed in niches high up on the outside of the temple.

On their way out of the temple compound, Deborah took some photos of the elaborate stone carvings adorning the gate, as the guide talked about their meaning in Balinese-Hindu mythology. But as they walked toward the next exhibit, Wayan was quietly shaking his head.

"That guy is just guessing. He didn't even recognize the carving of Bomo, above the gate. Bomo is the son of the earth god, and he protects the temple."

Whatever its name, that face above the gate was intriguing, and Deborah decided to make some sketches of it. The bulging eyes and fang-like teeth were fearsome, but the effect was softened by a field of blossoms surrounding the monstrous face. She decided to grab a quick lunch at the homestay and sit down with her new sketchbook.

Feeling secretive, she told Wayan only that she needed some down time that afternoon. Talking about it, she felt, would only jinx the artistic endeavor.

Yes, she had everything she needed. In addition to the sketchbook, Deborah had picked up pencils, marker pens, and a soft brush at the art supplies shop in Ubud. And a good eraser. It had been years since she had felt so well equipped. The smell of art supplies immediately brought to mind those wonderful afternoons when, starting around age 10, she would accompany her father on his "sketching breaks." One time they went to a museum in Philadelphia, but mostly they found themselves a spot in the Centennial Arboretum.

She decided to start by sketching the image sent by Teresa Campbell – the little offering basket, sitting on the ground. As excited as she was to sketch her butterfly — and the stone carvings — it seemed wiser to ease back into sketching with a less challenging assignment. And only as she drew the picture did it occur to her that this was an object she had seen almost everywhere: even on the ground in front of her own door.

On her second try, she produced a respectable drawing of the little basket with its marigold flowers.

small offering
basket
on the ground

Feeling pleased, Deborah made herself a cup of tea with the electric kettle, before settling in on her next assignment: the ornately carved stone temple gate, featuring the ogrish Bomo (if that's who it was).

It's surprisingly tricky, she soon learned, to sketch a monster: however grotesque its features, it needs to have some life on the page.

Bomo
guarding
a temple gate

Candace was coming back from doing some shopping, and she glimpsed Deborah hard at work, sitting at the table by her open door.

"So you're an artist, are you? I ought to have guessed!" She paused on her porch step. "I'd love to see what you're doing."

"I can show you when I have something finished, Candace. This is just practicing."

"Carry on, then." Candace nodded and went into her room, and immediately came out again.

"Deborah! You really need to see the art museum, ARMA — especially the older work. They have some amazing drawings, all sorts of fantastic creatures . . . ."

Deborah put down her sketchbook and looked up. Of course! With all the musicians and stone carvers and basket weavers, there had to be amazing painters here as well.

"It's getting late to go there today, though," the practical Candace pointed out. "You want to go fresh in the morning, and get your money's worth on the admission ticket."

The ARMA Museum sat on its own curated landscape — much like the Elephant Cave, Bali Park, and even that restaurant. But this place was in the heart of Ubud, unexpectedly showcasing several acres of hills and gardens surrounding a stream. Deborah resisted the impulse to follow the winding paths and instead walked directly into the imposing brick building that housed the collection of traditional Balinese art.

By the time she was ready to leave, almost two hours later, she felt she had understood something important. The progression from room to room, and from the first floor to the second floor, showed clearly how the art of painting had transformed itself in Bali over the twentieth century.

The very first paintings were on sturdy cloth, in a limited palette of colors: burnt orange, green, blue, and black. Those early paintings were done in a cartoon-like style: they were line drawings with flat perspective, arranged in panels — much like a storyboard. They mainly depicted heroes, giants, and animals, to retell specific episodes in Balinese Hindu mythology. Painting had been done the same way for many decades, possibly for centuries, similarly to the way stained glass images in European cathedrals were used to portray important characters and stories.

In the next room, however, Western art has arrived in Bali. A few European artists discovered this haven of the arts early in the twentieth century, and by 1930 they had developed a new style of their own. Painting the tropical landscapes around them, they adapted the linearity of the Balinese style to create mesmerizing artworks.

And then, in the entire remainder of the museum, Deborah saw how Balinese artists had answered the Western artists' challenge. Far from rejecting the foreign style, they picked it up and ran with it. They began to paint what they saw around them — not only the landscape, with its villages and rice fields, but also individual workers, artists, dancers. They painted houses, animals, celebrations, often in minute detail. And although the Balinese artists each had their individual style, there was somehow an enveloping Balinese-ness about the entire collection.

Emerging from the museum, Deborah allowed herself half an hour to explore its gardens. But she needed to get back to her sketching. Her own efforts might seem paltry, but she was encouraged by the idea that capturing Bali on paper was an enterprise with a rich tradition.

Her first order of business, on reaching home, was to celebrate — in ink on paper — the new-found Wood Nymph butterfly.

This was a different kind of challenge. She had to set aside her academic standards: the goal was not to produce a technical illustration, with each body part clearly defined, but rather to capture the feeling that had drawn her to studying butterflies in the first place — these creatures that seemed lighter than air, and more decorative than anyone could have designed. A butterfly that belonged to Bali: her butterfly must *breathe*.

Tree Nymph
butterfly

Among all the false starts, she now had three sketches that she felt were good enough to share. She picked them up and went outside to knock on Candace's door.

"Just a sec, love, be right there."

Candace came to the door with a towel wrapped around her head. "I've just been taking care of my roots," she announced. "Oh, are these your drawings?"

Deborah held the drawings up for inspection.

"Well. These are marvellous, aren't they? Really good!" Candace looked at Deborah with new interest.

"Thanks, Candace, it's been so long since I've done any drawing, it feels good to get back to it."

She didn't fool herself, though. This was just a rehearsal for showing her drawings to Wayan.

Chapter 8

Teresa Campbell chose to squat. She was grateful that the nicely appointed restroom at the hotel provided that option — intended specifically for people coming from the Balinese countryside, like herself, for whom sitting on a porcelain throne does not inspire the requisite inner relaxation.

Emerging from the immaculate stall, she was less appreciative of the wall-sized mirror that confronted her next to the sink. It had been several years since she had had a good look at herself below the shoulders, and she was not pleased with the direction things seemed to be heading. And her frame had lost some height over the years — though not from stooping; she still had the upright spine of a trained dancer. But above the shoulders? Under this glaring illumination, better suited to an operating theater, all was wrinkled pouchiness.

Giving her image a rueful smile, she straightened her sarong-style cotton skirt, of a deep blue that (she was told) matched her eyes, tailor-made by a neighbor who supported her family with sewing.

Teresa made her way through the over-energetic air conditioning of the hotel restaurant. The invitation to meet Deborah had taken her quite by surprise. When she posted her response to #**bali**okay, she had no idea, of course, that the original post was by someone local — in Bali, in Ubud. It had pleased her to think that someone was taking seriously Bali's unique climate.

She easily guessed that the woman at the table nearest the window was Deborah — but who was the nice-looking Indonesian with her?

Wayan saw Teresa approaching the table and immediately stood to greet her.

71

"Ibu Tera, I am very pleased to meet you."

Teresa's thumbnail bio (posted on *LinkedIn*) had not rung a bell for him; but now, in person, Wayan recognized her as an expert on Balinese dance, a long-time resident of Ubud.

A young waiter held a chair for Teresa, as the three finished their introductions and handshakes. She turned and said something to him before taking her seat at the table.

"Ibu Teresa is a well-known dancer," Wayan informed Deborah. Teresa smiled patiently as she shook her head. She was no longer part of a dance troupe, she explained, although she remained involved: she still managed all their bookings and tours, and some of their social marketing.

Teresa then turned to Deborah. "I was curious," she told her, "to meet the person who launched this Bali mania." There was no hint of hostility in the remark but rather a tone of wonder, and Deborah responded by sharing her own puzzlement.

"It's completely weird, and it makes no sense to me, Teresa. Wayan has 20 years of data, showing a clear pattern of climate reversal, and nobody pays any attention. But this *butterfly!* All of a sudden, people take it as some kind of mystical sign." She shrugged and rolled her eyes.

"It seems clear that our technical reports all need more butterflies," Wayan suggested, laughing, as the waiter came back to place a glass of tea in front of Teresa.

At Deborah's suggestion, Wayan ordered a few dishes to share. "And *krupuk* of course!" Deborah interjected. She had not forgotten those crisp, savory puffs. With the menus disposed of, Wayan came to the point that had nagged at him for the past week.

"I was surprised, Ibu Tera, when Deborah found your message on Pict." He paused. "Just the photo of the daily offering, sitting on the ground. I had to wonder, maybe you saw some connection that we were missing?"

Teresa sipped her tea — not too hot or too sweet, exactly as she had requested — and then looked at them both. "Well, it's *all* connected, isn't it?" She paused. She placed the glass on the table, giving it her full attention, and then looked up again.

"Even a Buddhist can't live every day as if the world is connected. I can recognize that my tea was made from a living plant, tended by people I never met, and that it was prepared for me by some other people I don't know. But most days, I drink my tea without thinking for a minute about where it came from.

"But you don't have to be a Buddhist to try to think about the place you live in. I mean, the larger place, the whole place. For the Balinese, the place they live is this lovely island, and it is always somewhere in their minds, even when they are doing their daily work. Don't you think so?" she asked Wayan.

He nodded, and then laughed. "Maybe more so in my case, given my line of work!"

Teresa's gaze grew curious, and he explained.

"My research is mostly about the irrigation system, for wet rice agriculture. And I also monitor the climate factors that affect it — rainfall and temperature. So I am always looking at different pieces of the system, the channels and dikes, and the crop yields, and the associated plantings and the farming techniques. But to me" — he gave a modest shrug — "what I am looking at is really, always, our earth and our water."

"Exactly!" Teresa leaned back with a broad smile. "Earth and water. The two sacred elements of Bali."

Now Deborah was puzzled. "What about all the Balinese gods and heroes and demons, in all the paintings and carvings?" She had grown rather fond of Bomo, in her many efforts to draw his picture.

"I don't speak as an expert," Teresa said, "but only as an observer. I think of the gods and heroes as an important story-telling tradition that has shaped every Balinese art form, as you've noticed." She gave Deborah an appreciative nod. "But there is a religious understanding here that is even more ancient. Anthropologist used to describe it as *animism*, the belief in the spirits of everything from the ancestors to the natural world — trees, rocks, rivers.

"To me, though, it is not so different from Buddhism. These spirits are not separate things, they are all part of one spirit. As we are, of course, as well."

Appetizers had arrived, and Wayan passed around the plate of spring rolls. But instead of eating, he then folded his hands on the table.

"You are a very good observer, Ibu Tera. We do have a more ancient Balinese religion, as I'm sure you know: *agama tirta*, the religion of sacred water. And I agree, it is about the earth *and* the water. We need earth and water to be in harmony, to support all the living things in our world." He leaned back. "But I am still not clear about the meaning of your message."

"I did not mean to be mysterious, I'm sorry for that. Sometimes I forget that I think a bit differently. . . ."

"It is why we were eager to meet you!"

Teresa smiled. "I just thought of that small offering as a way to represent the Balinese way of life, the nearly constant awareness of the importance of earth and water. All the traditions and arts in Bali are offerings, aren't they? Dances, too: at every performance, and even at our practices, we always place an offering on the earth.

"It always impresses me that so much of what people do in Bali is meant to honor the natural world, the natural elements that support all our lives. And the lives of the butterflies, too."

Deborah gladly accepted Wayan's offer to take her home, after the lunch. It would give her the opportunity to show him her better drawings.

"What did you think of Ibu Teresa?" she asked him, as they walked to the motorbike.

"I would say, she is the *opposite* of a silly woman." Wayan smiled. "We see a lot of foreign tourists, and many of them are what you could call silly women. They go home with their pictures and souvenirs, but they were never really here at all."

When they arrived at Ibu Made's homestay, Deborah got off the bike and stood directly in front of it. "Wayan, I have something to show you inside. It won't take long, and I'll ask Ibu Made to make us some coffee."

He parked the bike and followed her through the gate and up to the porch outside her room. After seating him in the large rattan chair, Deborah went inside to gather up her best drawings. She placed them on the table and went off to the kitchen to ask for coffee. Showing her drawings had always made her nervous.

As she came back up the porch steps, Wayan gave her a big smile. "Now I see it — why you fit so well here in Bali!" He was holding, carefully, her sketch of Bomo.

"Any time you walk down the street in Ubud, half the people you see are some type of artist. They paint, they carve masks, they play music or dance. If they have enough time to do those things. And you are the same; you are an *artist* as well as a scientist."

Deborah felt him looking at her with new appreciation — enough to make her blush all over again.

It came as a surprise, and an unexpected honor, to be invited to see a dance performance with Teresa that Friday: she should come for dinner and then stay overnight, as the performance would be quite late. Teresa gave her contact information for a driver she knew, Pak Mario.

Pak Mario turned out to be an excellent tour guide, ready to talk about everything they passed and happy to answer questions. In turn, he asked whether Deborah had seen some Balinese dances. He seemed puzzled when she said she had not.

"Most of the people who visit go there to see the history of Balinese dance. This is where some of the traditions were born!"

"You mean, the dancers are still making up new traditions?"

"Absolutely! I was named after one of the greatest. Over a hundred years ago, in the 1920s, Mario created a spectacular solo dance called kebyar. Now, all the male dancers have to learn it."

The driver pointed out a new mosque, one of several built in the area over the past few years. "We are mostly Hindu, but that doesn't mean there can't be other religions here. They also have respect for our religion, so I should be able to respect theirs."

Pak Mario went on to explain that Teresa's house was part of a large compound, with a huge carved gate and many steps. The owner, a famous dance teacher, hosted dance performances there almost every Friday night, and the dancers would make their entrance into the courtyard down the steps inside the gate. "And they all have to be strong dancers, to dance down those steep steps."

He guessed that Deborah would be staying at Teresa's house. "It's nicer than a hotel," he said, "although we don't have any hotel around here. The only thing is," he grinned into the rearview mirror, "if you don't like the dance performance, you will have no place to hide!"

The brick-walled compound was indeed large, with a high, imposing central gate. Deborah immediately saw how demanding it must be for dancers to make an entrance through that gate, as she carefully picked her way down the steep steps. Spread below her was, of course, the courtyard, much larger than Nyoman's. There was a pavilion set on one side of the courtyard, rather than in the center, and a gleaming gamelan set visible inside it. Rows of plastic chairs — still empty, thankfully — filled half of the central space, facing not toward the gamelan but outward toward the gate, as if watching her awkward entrance.

Teresa emerged from a house behind the gamelan pavilion, followed by two young girls, dancing in their eagerness to see the visitor.

"Deborah, I'm so glad you could come. Any trouble along the way? Come, I want to introduce you to Ibu Sutami, the director of the dance company." She directed the larger of the two girls to take Deborah's travel case back to the house, and the smaller girl soon scampered off, following her friend.

As they walked, Teresa explained.

"This place has been a dance center for five generations. Of course, it has grown over the years. Ibu Sutami is the one who added the dorm house for resident students, mainly for kids whose families are under stress. We have five dorm kids right now, all girls."

The two girls joined them again and immediately started off ahead. Climbing the steps of one of the houses, they began calling out.

Ibu Sutami came to the door with a smile. She said something to the girls, who dashed off again.

"Please come in," she said to her visitors.

Teresa introduced Deborah, and they entered the small living room, comfortably furnished with a sofa and armchairs. A glass-fronted cabinet displayed photos and other treasures.

"I'm very grateful to Teresa for hosting me," Deborah said as they took their seats. "It will be wonderful to see the dance performance, the first one I've seen since I've been here."

Ibu Sutami smiled again — tolerantly, it seemed to Deborah. She could suddenly see how strange it must seem, that someone could be in Bali for over a week and not see any dances!

An older woman came from a back room carrying a tray, with glasses of tea that (as Deborah had already learned) would be sweet. As she placed a glass in front of Teresa, she said something to her. Teresa laughed and explained, "Mine is not-too-sweet."

Ibu Sutami pointed out a framed photograph on the wall, a black and white portrait. "That is my great-grandfather. He trained some of the greatest dancers. I can show you their pictures, when we see the rest of the compound."

Teresa asked a few questions about that evening's performance, as some children clustered at the open door to stare at the visitor. After a few minutes, Ibu Sutami stood up.

"Let me show you our little photo gallery," she said, ushering her guests to the door as she shooed the children out of the way.

Following their tour of the dance pavilion and its photo gallery, Teresa led Deborah past the rows of chairs to a sheltered side pavilion, where a table had been set for three. A covered glass of tea sat at each place, and a young man was placing a tray on a low side table. Teresa introduced him as Ibu Sutami's son, Dewo, who helped manage the school. Deborah was delighted to see that the dishes on the tray included a bowl of *krupuk*.

"I remembered that *krupuk* is one of your favorites," said Teresa (who didn't miss much). "Actually, it's a favorite with just about everyone." She placed the appetizers on the table, and they took their seats.

They had just begun their soup, a deliciousy spicy clear broth, when they were joined by an English woman, probably in her late fifties, who dropped herself into the third chair and helped herself to a bowl from the serving tray. Teresa introduced her as her partner, Heather — a plant specialist, who knows all the traditional Balinese medicines and a lot more.

Deborah soon felt comfortable enough to ask her hosts whether they encounter any hostility, in their small town in Bali. Teresa laughed.

"It's okay, we're just the crazy old aunties!"

Heather put in, "Mind, now, it might be a bit different if we were Balinese."

Teresa nodded as she finished her soup. "Yes — even today."

The three foreign ladies, having finished their dinner, came out into the courtyard. Many of the plastic seats now had occupants, and the number of children cavorting around had multiplied. Teresa pointed out three reserved seats in the front row.

Deborah noticed people coming in through a side door; they were stopping at a nearby table, where an elderly gentleman was selling tickets. Deborah asked Teresa if she should buy a ticket.

"No, you are our guest. But donations are always appreciated, of course."

Deborah excused herself to join the group at the ticket table, wanting to make a donation before it slipped her mind. Coming back to her seat, she had to dodge a couple of women carrying woven trays of sweets and snacks for sale.

Almost every chair was full when Ibu Sutami came out to introduce the performance. The program began with a couple of gamelan pieces. Then came a short Welcome Dance: a group of six girls entered not from the stairs but from the back of the courtyard, each holding a small bowl of flowers. Deborah was charmed; she took a lot of pictures of the lead dancer, who she judged to be at most fifteen (a challenge to sketch!). The dancers' movements were like visual representations of the percussive gamelan notes — sharp, precise transitions from one highly stylized posture to the next. The girls' arms and hands could have been separately animated creatures, as they alternately stretched, swooped, and froze in position. The dancers finished by plucking, still in unison, a few flower petals from their bowls and tossing them out toward the audience.

"That was the traditional part of the evening," Teresa told Deborah, during the applause. "The next part is a new creation, a world premiere in fact. Traditionally, men and women have distinct dance styles, but this piece combines them."

As they waited, Deborah commented on the dancers' offering of flowers.

Balinese dancer with offering. Welcome Dance.

"Those flower petals are to welcome our guests," Teresa explained. "The dance itself serves as an offering to the natural world."

The gamelan came to life with a sharp clang, and one by one, dancers appeared in the narrow doorway at the top of the entrance stairs. Each was wearing a bright-colored leotard, bound at the hips with an equally bright gilded sash — men and women dancers costumed alike. As each dancer entered the doorway, they created a silhouette shape that moved and stretched in place; each dancer slowly moved down one step, and then another. As the gamelan shifted to a quicker tempo, the entire group of nine dancers stood arrayed on the steps as if suddenly frozen; and then, with athletic control, the dancers switched places a few times, before launching themselves, as a group, into the performance space.

The entire piece lasted around ten minutes, and Deborah felt she could have watched it all over again. Most of the audience was on their feet, applauding. Ibu Sutami stepped forward to bring the group back for a bow, and as the audience quieted down, she introduced the final dance. Teresa translated for Deborah: this dance was taken from the Ramayana epic — Hanoman, the monkey general, leading his army.

Cued by a gamelan introduction, the monkey general leaped to center stage and faced the audience, comical in his hairy gray mask. As he finished an acrobatic solo performance, to laughter and applause, he gestured right and left to bring out his troops: a small army of children, each dancing with fluid precision.

Following breakfast, Teresa invited Deborah to join her for her morning walk. "Then, if you feel like it, you can have a peek at the Saturday dance practice. It's the younger students in the morning."

Their walk took them along a country road, past irrigated fields that sparkled in the morning sun. A couple of smallish dogs attended them, probably hoping there would be scraps of food.

Deborah asked Teresa whether she was writing anything now, as a dancer or as an anthropologist.

"I was a writer until I became a Buddhist," Teresa answered simply. "I have not yet arrived at a Buddhist mode of writing."

"What do you think you would want to write about?" Deborah asked.

"I've become interested in the idea of evolution. I think that our current thinking is much more aware that the unit of evolution — certainly for humans — is not the individual but rather the social unit, the family or the community. To take one example, human life span is much longer than the reproductive lifetime. I think it would be safe to say that humans are the *grandparent species:* that is, the social groups that had a living grandparent generation would have enjoyed an evolutionary advantage. These old folks are not reproducing — but they are *producing.* And they share their decades of knowledge with the group." They walked a bit in silence. "Come to think of it, this may be something we share with elephants."

They had arrived at a little roadside shop; this was, Teresa explained, her marker to turn back toward home.

"Another example is the gay subpopulation. I can think of several potential evolutionary benefits to a neolithic community that includes some individuals who are not engaged in creating and caring for families of their own. Those people can spend their energies on inventing, or storytelling, or creating art.

"And who should guard the women and children, when the men go off hunting? Well, it seems to me, the perfect candidate would be a man who has no interest in having sex with the women."

Teresa stopped walking to think. "I wouldn't know how to write about all that, without sounding like special pleading. As an elderly lesbian, I mean."

Arriving back at the compound, they could see the dance class in progress. Most of the plastic chairs had been stacked at the sides of the gamelan pavilion, and the courtyard was now a dance school. Some women sat on one row of chairs, no doubt mothers of the students. In the center of the courtyard space, the teacher was leading the younger dancers in a sequence of steps. Two young women were assisting, by moving among the students to correct the position of hands or feet.

As they entered the courtyard, the teacher came over with a smile and invited Deborah to join the class. Deborah, horrified, simply shook her head before managing a proper "No, thank you." The poses looked quite impossible, elbows lifted high and hips curving out to one side. She quickly took a seat to watch. She recognized the two young girls who had carried her bag. In the front row of students was the lead dancer of the Welcome Dance — looking even younger without her dance makeup. When the class took a break, Deborah took the opportunity to tell her, "Thank you, it was a beautiful dance." She then managed to dredge up one of the few words of Indonesian she had learned: "Bagus!" (*ba*-GUSS). She was rewarded with a shy grin.

Teresa brought Deborah back to her house for a quick tea break, before her taxi was due to arrive. Deborah struggled to express her thanks, which Teresa smilingly waved away. "It's always good to invite a new perspective on the things we have learned to take for granted," she said. "Your visit has been perfect in that regard."

Feeling even more awkward, Deborah plunged ahead.

"I'm embarrassed to ask this, Teresa, but I don't even know whether Wayan is married . . ."

It had honestly not occurred to Deborah to check for a wedding ring. But do Balinese people even wear them?

"I tend to think he's not married," Teresa answered. "But if I understand the thrust of your question, I would also guess that he is far too ethical to court a non-Balinese — even if his family has no objection." She put down her tea and sat back. "It's still true, you know, that women in Bali tend to lead restricted lives, once they join the husband's family. Someone like Wayan would be acutely aware of what he would be asking of his wife." Then she smiled. "But I'm curious, too. I can ask some friends who should know."

"You won't say anything about *me*, will you, Teresa?"

Teresa's smile became a chuckle. "No need to worry. Buddhism discourages idle gossip."

Chapter 9

Returning to Ibu Made's guest house felt like coming home, after that one night away. Deborah was eager to get out her sketchbook, eager to make an attempt at drawing the young dancer; but first she would treat herself to an outdoor shower.

Earth and water: water flowing over her own body and into the earth. Maybe this shower was also a kind of offering?

No, she decided. Not at all. An offering has to have an *intention* behind it, and an effort. Like a dance. Like an offering of marigold petals.

But standing in the shower, in the brilliant sunlight that streamed in through the bamboo screen, seemed to make things clearer. Exploring Bali and its traditions did not mean she was being a tourist, Deborah told herself. This new kind of research was just as important, in its own way, as recording her butterfly sightings.

A feeling of clarity, a new energy, stayed with her as she sat down with her sketchbook to tackle her dance photos. She had no hope of conveying the dancer's movement, she realized — but she could try to capture her own response to watching the dedicated young dancer.

After working for an hour, Deborah could see some real progress. She picked up her phone to take photos of the more successful sketches, including the one she was still working on. And there was a new message from Wayan, asking how her visit had gone. By way of answer, her fingers typed out a request: could they make another trip to some rice fields?

Later that afternoon, as they walked along the dikes between the fields, Deborah asked Wayan to explain what Teresa had been saying, back at the restaurant, about the importance of earth and water for Balinese people.

"For farmers," he began, "earth and water are everything. And we show that we understand their importance when we place our offerings at the field. One offering goes above the ground, on the stone shrine, for the rain we need. One offering goes onto the earth. We are thanking the earth, every day. And we hope that the earth accepts our offering and our thanks."

They walked the length of the next field in silence. Finally, Deborah asked her question.

"Wayan, would you ever *know* whether the offerings have been accepted?"

"Maybe we can't really know. But it is true that earth and water have always been treated with the utmost respect in Bali. And maybe it's also true that *they return that respect to Bali.*"

"You mean — by keeping agriculture healthy? By keeping the rain and the temperatures normal?"

Wayan stopped walking and faced her. "I don't know what to think. And neither does anyone else. But what you just said does seem to explain the situation — and there's nothing else that does."

Teresa was as good as her word. She texted Deborah that she would be in town the next day, and could they have lunch? She suggested a place known for its clear fish soup. Deborah was happy to see her and, at the same time, a bit nervous about what she might learn.

As she was going out the door to meet Teresa, Deborah had an inspired thought. She would give Teresa one of her better dancer sketches, as a gift for Ibu Sutami. Art as offering, yes — even art that was not very polished. Carrying the drawing in her tote bag made her feel somehow better prepared for this conversation.

Almost as soon as she sat down, Teresa put her hand on Deborah's and met her eyes.

"Wayan was never married. There was an engagement years ago, but his fiancee tragically died in a traffic accident. Some people were quick to say that it was not just bad luck but bad karma. Who knows what he himself might have thought? People find ways to blame themselves, don't they. He was certainly devastated, according to everyone who knows the family. For whatever reason, he has stayed unattached."

Deborah nodded, thoughtful. She took a breath and exhaled slowly.

"Thank you, Teresa. Even just as his friend, it's something I felt I needed to know."

While they waited for their soup, Deborah broached that other puzzle that was occupying her mind.

"Yesterday Wayan and I talked about your idea, about earth and water in Bali. And I think he is beginning to think that this is the best explanation for his climate findings — that the Balinese show respect to the earth, with the daily offerings, and the earth shows respect to Bali."

Teresa said nothing, and then slowly nodded her head.

"Teresa, am I correct that this was the meaning behind your very first message, when you sent me that photo of an offering? That the Balinese practice of placing offerings on the earth might actually play a role in preserving its *climate*?"

Sleep was not going to happen. During the day, it was possible to become absorbed in doing her work, or visiting a gallery, or making her sketches. But at night there was nothing to push aside the big, heavy thoughts about Bali mania.

Two big thoughts.

1) Something that she, personally, launched — #**bali**okay — had produced a seemingly world-wide overreaction.

2) She, Deborah Morrison, along with just two other people, had a glimmering of insight into the mystery of Bali's "throw-back" climate.

Scientists are trained to share their findings, she reflected. Even an untested hypothesis should be shared, to allow others to try to disprove it.

But now, she had an untested (and maybe untestable) hypothesis that seemed too . . . too flaky even to mention aloud, let alone publish.

The middle of the night can feel very alone. Deborah picked up her phone. In New York, it was lunchtime! She opened WhatsApp to call Cecily. It would be good to hear her cheerful voice, to talk about things that had nothing to do with Bali.

Cecily's voice did sound cheerful, though a bit breathless, as if walking. "Aunt Deb! I definitely wanted to talk to you!"

"Me too. How are things on your little island?"

Cecily laughed. "Mostly the same. But I have a new job! Still in the publishing racket." She paused. "I don't know if you will approve, though."

"Why wouldn't I approve? Are you publishing hate manifestos or something?"

Cecily laughed again. "Could be interesting, but no. Actually, you could say we're not actually *publishing* at all."

"I can guess. You do tweeting!"

"You're getting close, Aunt Deb. I'll be doing editing for Reedy. We only publish our books online."

Deborah gave a dramatic sigh.

"Welcome to the dark side of progress," she said.

Deborah hadn't spoken with Wayan since that second walk in the rice fields, two days ago. She felt that things were getting complicated, somehow, and not in a boy-meets-girl sort of way.

Wayan was someone she liked and respected. She even felt close to him, maybe closer than she liked to admit. But now, it seemed, they were *partners*: now, there was something important that they shared, something weird and confusing. She didn't want to have to think about it. And that meant that she didn't want to think about Wayan, either.

Of course, her brain went there anyway, even in daytime.

Wayan had told her, as they finished their walk in the rice fields, that he had absolutely no interest in presenting this "hypothesis" anywhere. It was crystal clear, he said, that it would have no impact whatsoever — except that it would probably put an end to his professional consulting work.

So now, had this weird hypothesis become *her* responsibility?

Deborah's daytime brain quickly squelched that thought. There was no chance for a scientific publication on the subject, even if she wanted to submit such an article. This hypothesis was far outside her field of expertise — unless you were going to define the butterfly habitat to include the spirit world.

Well, at least she could talk to *herself*, she decided. She would try to sketch out this hypothesis in some way that made sense to her. As if writing a blog, for an audience of just one confused individual. "Earth Logic," she called it. And she began to write:

> "Our environment consists of more than the things we can see . . . ."

Over the next three days, Deborah made additions and revisions to her private "blog," her earth journal. And on the third day, she suddenly had an urge to share it. So, that evening, she called Cecily, who answered immediately.

"Hey, how are your butterflies, Aunt Deb?"

"The butterflies are okay. Actually, kind of better than okay."

"What do you mean?"

"Tell you what. I'd really like you to read what I've been writing — it's not at all technical, I promise."

"Okay."

"But I'd prefer if you don't show it or share it with anyone. Not even that cute husband of yours."

"No problem, Aunt Deb. Butterflies aren't really his thing."

"I have to warn you, Cecily, there's a chance it will blow your mind."

Deborah had been doing more with her days than blog-writing. She had hired Mario, the taxi driver, to take her to some of the field sites she had mapped out with Wayan, and she was rewarded with a few more sightings. She wrote up her field notes, complete with an inventory of associated plants, butterflies, and other relevant insects. And of course, the sites that came up empty also had to be carefully recorded, in similar detail.

As much as she enjoyed working on her own, she was increasingly aware of a missing presence. She phoned Wayan.

"Hello, Deborah!" His voice sounded delighted.

"I just wanted to give you a progress report," she began, but he didn't give her time to finish.

"Can we have dinner this evening?" he asked. "I can pick you up around seven?"

They had dinner in the same hotel restaurant where they had met Teresa. The food was good there; and it was better for conversation than most other places, where your chair would be right next to someone else's table. He had dressed up, in a crisply decorative batik shirt.

They had finished dinner and were waiting for their coffee. Deborah pulled up her fieldwork tracking map on her phone, to show Wayan the sites she had visited. It was beginning to feel like good progress, she told him; she would soon have results substantial enough to write up. And that field report would then be the basis for comparison with other regional Southeast Asian findings.

She told Wayan about Stefan's fieldwork in the region, as one of the most meticulous researchers in their field. "He was very excited for me to get the real findings for Bali," she said, as the waiter served their coffee.

"Have you told Stefan what you've found so far?" he asked, when the waiter had left.

"Not yet," she shook her head. "I'll send him my report for his comments, when it's ready."

Wayan smiled at her. "Good, I was worried."

It took Deborah a minute to understand what he meant, and then (naturally!) she found herself blushing once again. Wayan reached across the table to take her hand.

"Deborah, listen. I want to be the person that you talk to, about your work and anything else. Does that make me selfish?" He waited for an answer, and then released her hand. "I know it sounds over-dramatic, but it has been ten years since I've wanted to share everything with another person."

She sipped her espresso, unable to say anything.

Wayan continued. "I knew that you were that person almost right away. But I also know that it's not easy for an outsider to make their home here in Bali. I've been thinking about nothing else for the past week." He looked down at his hands. "You know that I care about our traditions; they mean a lot to me. But traditions can be prejudices, sometimes. And that is not how I want to live my life, ever — or let other people live my life for me."

Deborah put down her cup and looked up at him. She took a deep breath.

"When I saw Teresa, I asked her to find out something more about you," she confessed. "She told me about your engagement, and the tragedy."

"It was ten years ago." He nodded his head slowly. "In my mind, it seemed like ten days instead of ten years. Until I met you."

Now Deborah reached across to take his hand in hers. All she could say was, "Thank you."

Walking outside together, afterward, felt very different from when they arrived. They stood still for a few minutes, side by side, without speaking. And then, Deborah began to laugh. Relief flooded in, and she could hardly speak.

"I'm sorry," she gasped. Then, to his puzzled look, she explained, "I was about to invite you back to my place — to see my new *sketches*!" She suppressed a giggle. "I feel like I'm in a cartoon, it's such an old joke!"

Wayan said nothing as he put his arm around her and drew her closer. Deborah raised her face to his, inviting a first, and very memorable, kiss.

As their motorbike approached Ibu Made's gate, it stopped a few feet earlier, at the side of the road. Deborah got off so that Wayan could park the bike. She was pleased to see, as they entered the gate, that no one was around. And immediately, she was annoyed with herself that it should matter.

As they came into her room, she started to switch on the light but stopped herself and turned around. And then, the only thing that mattered — for quite a while — was that someone had taken someone else into their arms.

Morning was for conversation, too. Deborah made them some tea, with the electric kettle.

"Is there some way," she asked him, "that people here remember someone they've lost? Are there offerings that you make?"

Wayan shook his head. "Offerings are for the ancestors of the family," he explained. "At the cremation, of course, there are always many offerings, but they are not for the person."

"Well, maybe there needs to be a new tradition," she said. "Maybe, make an offering as a remembrance. At some very special place."

Wayan looked thoughtful. "I wanted to take you there anyway, but it never seemed to be the right time. Just a little wooden bridge, between two fields." He looked up at her. "And it *is* special, at sunset."

"Let's do it, then. Tomorrow, at sunset."

Wayan shook his head again. "I wouldn't know how to invent an offering. Or what words to say."

"How do you say, 'I miss you,' in Balinese?"

"I will try to figure it out!" With a quiet laugh, he reached out for her hand, and she gave his hand an encouraging return squeeze.

Keeping her hand in his, Wayan grew solemn again. He began to talk about that dream that had so disturbed him, on his trip to Kuala Lumpur. His voice was so quiet that she leaned in to hear the words.

"I really never gave much thought to the offerings we make, even though they are part of every farmer's life. Everyone's life, of course. But then, in my dream, I was horrified to see them disappear like that: the offerings for the family shrine were dissolving." He blinked the image away. "It was maybe even worse to see the shrine itself change shape and become distorted. It felt — threatening."

Deborah nodded, and drew her hand gently back. She got up and went over to her cabinet, and came back with the sketchbook.

"Maybe that's why I had so much trouble trying to draw this shrine," she said, with a rueful smile. "I still need to start over again."

Wayan took the sketchbook opened to the shrine drawing.

"It needs to be twice as tall, and also darker, to be like the one in my dream." He grinned up at her. "And it has to lean closer *in*, instead of leaning *away*."

Carved
Stone
Shrine

Chapter 10

Deborah's butterfly, with its celebratory **#bali**okay hashtag, was still circling the globe three weeks later. Bali was well known, of course, as a getaway destination; but this butterfly seemed to promise something more than a getaway. It came to represent a kind of *salvation*, in the public imagination — a sign that the world might be okay. Almost like Noah's dove, carrying the olive twig.

Bali soon became a staple topic of talk shows. It was now routinely referred to as "Bali OK" (as if it were a town in Oklahoma, rather than an island of Indonesia). For most of the talking heads, Bali was *the* place to be. And when viewers got the idea that, somewhere on our poor planet, things were the way they used to be — that, somewhere, you could go back in time, maybe 20 years — it was more than just a sensation or a fad. It was a tease; it was a taste.

Up to now, climate change around the world had spurred migration flows from the Global South to Global North — from the Third World to the First World. But before too long, "Bali OK" began to inspire migration in a new direction. If *you* were working remotely, wouldn't you prefer to do it from Bali? For athletes, Bali became the place to do "relief training," free of noxious atmospheric effects. Tourism had a different flavor, now: people came to Bali not for the arts, or even the beaches. Many of the new migrants came to sense their own survival. These days, any decent climate consultant was supposed to get you to Bali — whatever it took.

Cecily's mind was indeed blown. Maybe because of her immersion in yoga, she found that *Earth Logic* made perfect sense.

> The repetition of small-scale activities, performed by thousands of people over hundreds of years, has apparently created a kind of energy shift; and this, in turn, has had profound effects on local atmospheric processes.

But then, a minute later, she would kind of shake herself and go, *Whaaat*? She knew she needed to discuss *Earth Logic* with Mattias. She called Deborah.

"Deborah, this is fantastic!" She began to read Deborah's words back to her:

> As we begin to find ways to express appreciation for our planet, especially through small, daily actions to honor our earth and water, we can begin to focus our minds on what it is that we most value.
> And from that awareness we can develop effective, larger-scale actions, to help to heal the earth, water, and air that sustain us.

"Can I share this with Mattias? He's the other half of my brain."

Deborah laughed. "Sure," she said. "Half of *my* brain is in someone else's head, too."

Oh, wow. For Cecily, this was actually bigger news than the idea for healing the planet. She knew, of course, that her Aunt Deb had found a soulmate in Bali, and that *Earth Logic* was their brainchild. But to hear her embrace the new relationship, in the same way that Cecily thought of Mattias, came as an unexpected thrill.

She brought her wandering thoughts back to the big question: How to bring Earth Logic into public awareness? Even though her job was in publishing, in fact Cecily's own media experience was limited to posting her honeymoon album on Pict — and having that single image take off. Seeing her beautiful butterfly flit around the world had been a heady experience. That one photo had been zoomed, filtered, cartooned, and animated; somebody had even made it into a hologram, that users could "adopt." It felt as if she were riding some slow-motion roller coaster.

But this was different, and a bit scary. Cecily felt a new sympathy for that butterfly.

Indonesia at first welcomed this crazy new flow of tourists. They had already experienced a dramatic uptick in Australian immigration in the wake of the almost continent-wide wildfires of the 2020s, spurring such developments as the condo-mall enclave generally known as AussieTown. And they knew that all the new foreign spending — in spite of some inevitable cultural friction — was helping to sustain Bali's cultural traditions, while also (not incidentally) producing tax revenue. Accordingly, a beneficent Ministry of Immigration issued a surprising number of long-term visas and permanent residencies.

The Governor of Bali, too, recognized the economic benefits of tourism; but before long she began to have serious concerns about an upward trend that showed no signs of leveling off. Ibu Ketut (as she was generally called) called her senior team together to develop a policy response.

Pak Ika was ready; he had been ready ever since he saw #**bali**okay trending on social media. So now, he armed himself for the Governor's meeting with the organizational chart he had drawn up, showing all the national and regional governmental agencies and offices that play a role in immigration. And, prominently at the lower right, labeled in red, was his proposed addition, a shiny new unit: the Immigration Permitting Office for Bali.

One learns patience, serving in any bureaucratic role. The meeting had been going on for over an hour, as each official around the (sustainable teak) table expounded on the (obvious) potential perils and advantages of doing business as usual, in the face of this unprecedented pressure of tourism and immigration. Ibu Ketut was looking around the table, preparing to wrap things up, when Pak Ika asked her permission to present a *proposal*. With all eyes on him, and with careful deliberation, he leaned down to bring out of his briefcase eight copies of his proposed organization chart, which he passed around.

"Ibu Governor, it is clear to all of us that Bali could become unrecognizable if we fail to develop a strategy to monitor and respond to trends in immigration, without further delay. Bali cannot always rely on New Jakarta to provide a timely response on immigration policy questions." (Indonesia's capital, Jakarta, had been moved to a different city more than a decade ago to avoid flooding, but the new name had never caught on.) "We will need to manage our own immigration and tourism processes. And that will require a separate authority: the Immigration Permitting Office for Bali."

There was silence, followed by grumbling and headshaking around the table. One or two officials voiced the general objection to the plan, arguing that this proposal would duplicate existing functions — no doubt sensing, correctly, that Ika had positioned himself nicely to head up this new unit.

And then Pak Ika brought out his second chart: *Meteorological Trends for Bali in the Context of Southeast Asia Weather Patterns, 2016-2036: Temperature.* And there it was, plain to see — Bali's orange line, with its surprising downward trend, meticulously drawn by scientists. Pak Ika was sure (he confided) that everyone present would understand the significance of Bali's unique weather pattern: one must expect that the demand for visas would only increase over time.

Governor Ketut was persuaded. However, decisions about immigration administration did not rest with her. She ended the meeting without giving her opinion on the proposal. Within the following week, however, she arranged for a smaller team to accompany her to New Jakarta (or NewJak, as it was often, clumsily, shortened). They would present a plan to the Ministry of Home Affairs on the delicate matter of decentralizing certain aspects of immigration. More specifically, their proposal would establish a visa system for Bali. A separate visa would be required to enter Bali, in additon to the visa for Indonesia.

Negotiation at the Ministry proved easier than she had expected, after one of her team proposed also instituting a separate visa process for travelers *from all the other islands of Indonesia*. Most of the old perks of government office had been dismantled over the years, and it is possible that the immigration officials in New Jakarta recognized, and appreciated, a new perk when they saw it.

And so it was, that Pak Ika soon received a new title: Director General for Immigration in the Province of Bali.

The spike in demand affected not only tourist visas. Increasing numbers of westerners were applying for an Indonesian residency permit, to allow them to live in Bali. Of course, once Bali had established its own immigration bureaucracy, that process became more difficult. Any extended visa for Bali now required the applicant to be sponsored by a local *banjar* (a requirement which fostered, naturally enough, a brand new income stream for the larger *banjars*).

This highly sought-after residency permit would soon become known as the "Greener Card."

Deborah would have said that she was pretty well prepared, by now, for almost any kind of reaction to her butterfly posting. That is, until she answered a random phone call that claimed to be from the office of the Climate Czar.

The crisp female voice on the phone began by asking to confirm who she was. After these preliminaries came a request: would she share her data with their office?

"Do you mean, my field notes on butterflies?"

"Exactly. How much time do those records cover?"

"About a month of fieldwork."

The voice explained a procedure for securely uploading to their data system, and then ended the call with a rather perfunctory thank-you.

The very next day came a call from the Climate Czar himself, a Mr. Godfrey Kline. He wanted to know when Dr. Deborah Morrison would be back in the U.S., so he could invite her to give a briefing to his office: not only on her field data, but on whatever else she had observed during her Bali stay. And were there other scientists working there, that she could refer them to? Did she know anyone who was working specifically on the meteorological pattern around Bali, and its implications?

Deborah promised Mr. Kline that she would do some asking around. She realized instantly how pathetic that must sound. A month in Bali, amid all the hoopla about the Balinese microclimate, and it hadn't yet occurred to her to seek out a local expert?

As she anticipated, Wayan had no wish to be part of an official research agenda. However, he did give her permission to share his report. Except that he had changed the byline: instead of his own name, the byline now simply cited, "Meteorological Working Group, Province of Bali, Indonesia."

"This report is the gold standard," the deputy Climate Czar is telling his staff. "This gives locally recorded measurements, temperature and rainfall." The deputy's assistant is distributing copies around the room: *Meteorological Trends for Bali in the Context of Southeast Asia Weather Patterns, 2016-2036.*

"Assuming that the data are *reliable*," he continues, "this report shows a trend that nicely parallels the regional trends, from 2016 up to about 2025. But at that point, the data for Bali show an increasing divergence. Basically, *Bali returns to the* old *normal.*" He directs a staffer to prepare slides of the relevant charts from the report. He then assigns a small team to produce their own report on the data, for use at his briefing with the Czar later that week.

Two days later, that working team reports back with a draft — coupled with a caveat. They can find no academic citations to that Balinese report. "It seems odd, sir, that such a dramatic finding has not been cited anywhere."

"Moverover," another voice chimes in, "we have no names for the researchers or authors. Let alone bios."

"All right," the deputy sighs, clearly exasperated. "We can't cite a basically anonymous report. And we can't appear as the *first* citation to some random field report."

The deputy is scheduled to brief the Czar that afternoon. Now he reverts to Plan B: he buries that staff report, along with the original report from Bali, safely in his desk files. No need to take any chances on being overruled by the Czar's enthusiasm.

Then, as a long shot, he phones their contact person in Bali, Dr. Deborah Morrison. It's not yet midnight over there.

"Dr. Morrison? I'm calling in my capacity as the deputy to the Climate Czar, Dr. Godfrey Kline. We are hoping you can help us out by providing information about the author of the meteorological report on Bali — name, contact information, and if possible, a short bio or resume?"

Deborah is in fact wide awake at this point, but it seems wiser to sound sleepily confused. "Mmm, I guess I can try to get something for you. Thanks for calling." She clicks off the call.

The short conversation awakened Wayan as well. He reached an arm around Deborah's shoulder, as she stowed the phone back on the nightstand.

"Must be USAID," he muttered. "They never grasp the idea of time zones."

"Close," she yawned. "I'll tell you about it in the morning."

But her brain was not ready to let go of this new problem. Even a sweet cuddle didn't manage to turn off her concerns. As a scientist, she was relieved to think that Wayan's decades of data would be given due attention. Maybe his report would even have an influence on policy decisions. But — also as a scientist — she worried that the information would get sucked into some existing policy dispute that they knew nothing about. After all, this was a request from a government agency, not from some other scientist. And if the report did become a football, what would be the consequences for Wayan himself? Or for the two of them?

When morning came, it brought no new insights. Making the tea, Deborah told Wayan who it was that had phoned in the middle of the night.

"They have your report, and he was phoning to say thank you. *Not!*"

"What else do they want?" Wayan asked, knowing the answer.

"Name, bio, serial number."

"Serial ...?"

"I'm joking, that's only if you're captured by the enemy. They do want a phone number and everything." She put their cups on the table.

"Deborah, do you have any idea what they are planning to do with the report?"

"He didn't say. And honestly, even if he has a plan, there's no way to know what else will happen with it. At best it would just be a huge waste of time, if you have to deal with reporters from all over the world."

"So, you will just say you don't know?"

"Yes, for now. But, Wayan," she turned to look at his face. "What do *you* want to happen, with that report?"

"It's so simple. I wanted to share it with the community of climate scientists, so it would become part of the global databases. In a way, that's the opposite of giving it an official parade in Washington DC."

By the time of the scheduled briefing with his boss, the deputy has made a decision. That report will remain safely in his files.

"Sir," he begins, "we are running a reputational risk." You always need to start strong. "This Balinese study may have serious flaws, and there are no citations to it anywhere."

"Okay, so you're telling me to just ignore the data?"

"Well, sir, we *could* send a review team over there, to at least check out the data setup. And interview the researchers." The deputy hesitates. "However, it would probably not be possible to do that without attracting news coverage. Whatever we find in the end, the news story will claim that we're *endorsing* the report."

Czar Godfrey stands up and leans heavily over his broad desk. "Sometimes I flatter myself," he said, "that my qualifications for this job go beyond that pretty picture." His bushy eyebrows lift, to indicate the framed official portrait on the wall. "During my tenure, at any rate, we are not going to make important decisions by worrying about the *optics*." He emerges from behind the desk. "I have to admit, though, sending a review team would invite speculation in the press."

He walks his deputy to the door. "Why don't you send just *one* staffer, instead of a team. Under the radar."

The deputy nods, relieved to have secured some kind of review process. "I'll send Dan."

"This is kind of a diplomatic assignment," Godfrey observes.

"Dan's a bit prickly — okay, he can be abrasive. But he does have the best BS detector in the business."

Godfrey closes the door after his deputy, and he puts in a call to his squash partner, Joe — who happens to be the Director of USAID.

Growing up in Chino, California, Jose Medina had a promising career ahead of him as an opera singer until he went to UCLA, where he discovered his inner nerd, immersing himself in earth sciences and international studies. But his cultured baritone always has a starring role at the annual USAID holiday party, and it lends an operatic note, on occasion, to their squash matches.

"Joe! I need to get your read on a report we received that might be a bit sketchy. Nothing *corrupt*, as far as we know," he hastens to add. "Just maybe not a reliable data source."

"Sure. How urgent is this? I don't have a lot of free time before Friday's positioning document."

"Friday would be great. Come to my office whenever you close up shop. I'll still be here, we can have a drink."

"Joe, you folks are tracking the news stories about Bali, I'm sure." Joe merely chuckle-groans in reply. "Well, we weren't planning to get involved in it, either, but now there's a couple of things happening on that."

Joe's eyebrows go up, expectantly, while Godfrey, at the sideboard, pours two happy glasses.

"Cheers (I think)." He hands Joe a glass.

"First thing is that our own global data is showing a microclimate anomaly, exactly in south central Indonesia. My approach was going to be to just release the data giving the map coordinates, so it doesn't spark a media frenzy."

"Sure — no press conference, just a standard press release."

"But here's the second thing. All this media hype had to come from somewhere, and we tracked it back to a *lepidopterist*. She found a butterfly that actually shouldn't have survived climate change — in Bali."

"Okay. A butterfly."

"My job isn't to hide from data, it's to find what's out there. So, we contacted the lepidopterist and asked her for some research sources on climate, some meteorologists. And it turns out, the meteorological data is there, and it's stunning."

"So — *now* you need to hide from it?"

"First off, we can't verify the quality. We don't even have the names of the authors, so, of course, no bios. And there are *no* following citations! Ours would be the first citation. We can't do that."

"Godfrey, it strikes me that you have a bigger problem than verification. Once it's verified, even if it's as sound as Fort Knox, you publish this . . ."

"That is exactly what I need from you, Joe. How big is this impact going to be?"

Joe finished off his glass. "Let's talk again in a couple of days."

On the way home, Joe phones his assistant to set up a meeting with the Indonesian Ambassador. He'd been meaning for a while to get Ambassador Farid's thoughts on the Bali craze. And, more to the point, no one he knew would have a better handle on gauging potential impact.

Chapter 11

"Are you sure you want me to come with you?" Deborah asked.

"I *need* you to come with me," Wayan answered. This was true, though he wasn't sure exactly why. He knew that this offering was not meant as a "goodbye" to Murnia, who would always be somewhere in his thoughts. Maybe, he thought, this offering was about enlarging the circle. Deborah had shown him a way to honor Murnia's memory, and she, too, would always be part of his life.

After working for a good hour, sitting on Deborah's little porch, they had succeeded in creating three small offerings — three modest woven baskets, filled with flowers. He was spending most of his non-working hours there, now, and today they were going to place the special offering at the bridge. Ibu Made had shared a supply of bamboo leaves and marigold flowers, as well as some expert guidance, for very modest compensation. Wayan was embarrassed at not knowing exactly how to make these simple objects. He explained to Deborah that it was normally women who created them.

"Even the taxi driver — the offering he puts on his dashboard was made for him by his wife."

He reflected, also, that he might have asked his mother to do the honors, instead of Ibu Made. But he had not yet introduced Deborah to his family. Some unquestioned logic told him that introducing Deborah to Murnia was an essential first step.

Wayan took a different road than they had taken before. It was still daylight, with more than an hour until sunset. After maybe half an hour, he stopped, and they parked the motorbike next to an overgrown path.

"I should have brought a machete," he commented. "People need to settle, once and for all, who owns this field!"

Deborah led the way, glad to have worn her field boots and long-sleeved camp shirt: Wayan had warned her that the place might be rugged. After about ten minutes of walking (that felt a lot longer), they could hear the gurgle of a healthy stream quite nearby.

Wayan had already taken the lead, back where the tangle had begun to seem impassable. He breathed, "We're here!" before plunging ahead into a thicket. He tore the vines apart, and now Deborah could see the flow of water below. He took her hand as he stepped out ahead of her, and now her foot found a wooden bridge.

"I hope this thing isn't rotten," she said, stepping gingerly forward.

Once on the bridge, they had a clear view, free of vines. The stream was visible for a mile each way: it came toward them through a series of well-tended rice fields, beginning to churn just at the point where the land ownership evidently lapsed — where stones and roots had been left uncleared in the streambed. Downstream, the water found its way, once again, into a clear channel, through the recently harvested fields on either side.

Wayan lifted his backpack from his shoulder and carefully reached inside, bringing out one of the offering baskets. They had planned to place them at three points — one at each end of the bridge, and one in the middle. The water beneath them was already showing the pale rose tint of the sky.

Wayan looked at Deborah; taking her hand, he smiled. "I will do the first one myself," he said. He kneeled where he stood and placed the offering basket on the bridge. He then took from his backpack a stick of incense, and a lighter. He held the lit incense stick over the offering, waving the smoke gently upward with his other hand, as he said some quiet words, and then he placed the stick in the basket. He knelt for a few minutes, silently, and stood up.

"We place the second one at the other end of the bridge," he said.

He led, walking the few steps across the stream to where the bridge ended in another thicket of vines. The surface of the water gleamed a bright yellowish pink. Wayan brought out a second basket and incense stick, and he turned to face Deborah.

"Will you place the second offering, Deborah?"

She took the basket and kneeled on the bridge, placing it down before her with both hands as she had seen him do. Wayan lit the incense stick and handed it to her.

Deborah hadn't thought about this step, or about her role in the ritual. She took the incense stick and held it over the offering. Why were there tears coming? She blinked a few times, and she whispered, "Thank you for this blessing in my life."

Wayan helped her to her feet, and they walked back to the center of the bridge. Deborah turned to look upstream; the sky was already blending gold and deep rose, while the stream poured its echoing colors into the countryside. After watching for a moment, they knelt side by side. Wayan placed the third offering on the bridge, and he lit the third incense stick.

"This is for the earth and the water, and for the memory of Murnia," he said in English, and then paused. "And this is Deborah, who belongs here. With the earth and the water, and with me."

They stood up together, and Wayan kept Deborah's hand in his as they watched the enormous golden orb finish its journey to the horizon.

The walk back up the path was easier, mostly in silence. Getting onto the motorbike, Deborah felt a new swell of contentment; and, as they rode into the lingering violet light of the sunset, she put her head back with a laugh of pure joy. She still had one more message to convey: a silent farewell. *Jason, buh-bye.*

The Indonesian Chancery is one of the most beautiful historic buildings in Washington, a stone mass that dominates a corner near downtown Dupont Circle. The elaborately carved, Victorian-era mahogany paneling, paired with the frescoed and gilded ceilings and the Tiffany skylight, all seemed somehow appropriate, Joe thought, to represent the elaborate cultures of Indonesia.

Joe always liked having an excuse to visit. The appointment is set for the next day.

On the way over, he tells his driver that the Indonesians have made one major contribution to life in DC. "It actually improves your life, too, Paul. On a daily basis."

Paul gets that there's a joke coming, and he plays along. "How's that, Mr. Medina?"

"That nice shirt you're wearing? Ten years ago, that would have been the full-on, button-up, button-down shirt — with a jacket and tie. How would you feel about climbing into *that* every day?"

"Not too happy, sir. But I don't really think this shirt came from there."

"No. The point is, the Indonesian diplomats changed the whole style of DC. Men's summer shirts used to be limited to pastel plaids, just perfect for a spin on the yacht. And there were comfy polos for the golf course — no one was going to wear that stuff to the office, if it wasn't casual Friday. The shirts you and I have on right now are based on the batik shirts they've worn for decades in Jakarta. Solid fabric, dark colors. Short sleeves in summer, and patterns that are way too good to cover up with a jacket."

Joe concludes the mini-seminar, as Paul steers the SUV through the iron gate at the Embassy.

"Say, Paul, while you're waiting, why don't you check out that Moslem statue they've got out in front?"

Passing through the security annex and the hallway into the old mansion, Joe inhales the grandeur of the original ballroom. Embassy staff are stacking chairs from an earlier event; chandeliers and sconces everywhere are ablaze, picking out the gilded trim above the mahogany paneling. He is ushered toward the Ambassador's spacious office, which occupies a secluded section of the main floor.

Ambassador Farid (fa-REED) does not keep him waiting. A tall man with a ready smile, he has been nicknamed "Fred" by his friends in the U.S. Fred now radiates welcome, as if the two men have never had anything awkward to discuss. "Great to see you, Joe. I'm pretty sure your positioning exercise at USAID has kept you too busy to play squash."

"You're right about that. But my knees appreciate getting a break. The rest of me is still 30 years old, you know."

The ambassador ushers him to a leather armchair and takes one himself. "Joe, we all wonder how you manage that bit of magic!"

Joe simply smiles in reply, recognizing that this isn't the moment to launch into a lecture on healthy fats and carbs. He leans forward.

"Fred, I don't have any specific updates for you, but I'd really like to get your opinion on something. In a general way."

"Of course."

"It's about Bali."

"Not too surprising. I hear that Indonesia is going to become part of Bali one of these days." (It was a standing joke at the Embassy that, when folks don't know where Indonesia is, they often ask if it's in Bali.)

"Fred, we have some reporting that still needs to be vetted. But if it pans out, it will actually *confirm* all the internet buzz."

Farid's face doesn't change, but he sits a little straighter.

"It looks as though, initially, Bali was hit by all the well-known regional weather patterns, just like Java and Sulawesi. Generally, Bali showed all the same drops and bumps — until suddenly, it didn't anymore. About 10 or 15 years ago, I'm told. And now, Bali's *new* normal looks a lot like the *old* normal."

Farid says nothing. He gestures politely to the two cups of tea that have been quietly placed in front of them. And then he nods his head and smiles.

"You are right, Joe, as always. Thanks. We do need to take some time, on our side, to develop some strategy — before the internet gets its confirmation."

"We certainly want to be helpful. If you have any thoughts to share with us, you know where to find me." Joe stands up. "I never get out of the office these days."

Getting back into the car, Joe asks Paul what he thinks of the Moslem statue.

"If you say so, sir, but it doesn't look very Moslem to me. It's a woman, and she doesn't have a head scarf on. And she has extra arms."

"Bingo! You cracked the code, Paul. It's a *Hindu goddess*. At the embassy of a so-called *Moslem country*. I think they put up a Hindu statue to push back against the idea that Moslems are intolerant. Back when tolerance was still considered a good thing."

"That's pretty amazing," Paul agrees. "And by the way, sir, as long as we're keep everything straight . . ."

"Yeah?"

"I understand that Moslems don't do statues. Of people, anyway. It's against their religion."

Dan Munro had decided to route his travel through NewJak, instead of flying into the Bali international airport. He had a couple of people to catch up with at the U.S. Embassy; and besides, he was curious to see how much the new capital city had grown by now. The only other time he had been there was just a year after the big move, and not very much was in place.

Getting to the Embassy from the newly expanded airport was a breeze — a major benefit from his own point of view. On the ride into town, he was impressed by the number of high-rise hotels that had sprung up around the airport and at a few other strategic points along his route. He had booked a room for one night at a new hotel in town, one that was used by most of the American contractors.

Jody Echols, in the Econ section, was expecting him and had given his name to security. The guard at the desk checked his ID as he signed in, and then called Econ to send someone to escort Dan upstairs. While he waited, he studied the space. The building seemed small, for a post in a major country; but even so, he judged, it represented a massive investment. Building anything anywhere outside of Java must have entailed a significant cost multiplier.

Jody met them at the elevator. "Dan, it's great to see you! Not too many people come here instead of going to Bali."

"Still the boonies?"

"In a way. Most of the folks you need to talk to are right here, and it's a whole lot easier to get to see them than back in Jakarta." Jody steered them to his glass-fronted office.

"You were posted there in the twenties, right?"

"Right. We had just moved into our fancy-schmancy new building in downtown Jakarta when the final decision came down — close up shop and move to the new capital. I was lucky, though. I missed all the hassle when I got posted to Cairo."

"What did they do with the Jakarta building?"

"Same as the other embassies. A lot of the work still gets done there, that doesn't involve direct dealings with the Ministries."

"How bad is the flooding there, these days?"

"It's still seasonal, but it's impossible to get anywhere for a few months each year. People are basically telecommuting."

Jody ushered his guest to the practical gray microfiber sofa and seated himself in the matching easy chair. An assistant came in with a pitcher of water and poured two glasses.

"Something stronger?" Jody asked. "You've been traveling, what, 27 hours?"

"Yeah, Uncle Sam doesn't like to spring for supersonic. But I'm okay. Could use a cup of coffee, though. Can you call it Java here?" Jody laughed and nodded to his assistant.

"So, you're here to do some fact-finding? On climate?"

Dan leaned back and rubbed his eyes. "You could say that. We have this dramatic report of climate findings for the past 20 years. In Bali." He sat forward for emphasis. "And it doesn't look like anything else in the entire region."

"Can we get a copy at Econ?"

"I'll tell my boss you're interested. It hasn't been cleared for distribution at all, as far as I know. That's kind of my job — to find out who the heck did the research, and how reliable it is."

"Seriously, let me know what you find out. Obviously, this would have implications on the economic front. Does the Indonesian government have the report?"

"I can try to find that out as well."

It was just a short hop from NewJak to the international airport in Den Pasar, Bali. Dan had arranged to meet Prof. Morrison at the coffee shop of the biggest hotel in Ubud. The traffic in Bali was much worse than in New Jakarta, and he texted the professor that he'd get there a half-hour late.

Looking around the coffee shop, he surmised that she had not yet arrived, and he took a table (by habit) farthest from the plate glass windows. He told the server he was meeting someone.

"Excuse me, sir, are you Mr. Munro? Your party is waiting for you."

Grunting his acquiescence, Dan moved to join the young woman at her table next to the window — silently protesting, "They don't make professors like they used to."

"Glad to meet you, Ms. Morrison," he said aloud, shaking hands. "Excuse me, I meant *Professor* Morrison." He moved the menu aside, as he took his seat; he knew what he wanted.

Dan regarded the young woman across the table.

"Our office is very appreciative of your help, in providing climate data for this area." It was not Dan's habit to waste his time on small talk. "And my assignment is to provide some background for the data. I'm sure you will understand, Professor, that we can't use data that we can't verify."

Professor Morrison did not seem inclined to do much talking, but she nodded her head. A waiter arrived with a notepad, and she gave her order. Dan explained exactly how he liked his coffee.

"The most important thing," he continued, "is to get in touch with the principal researchers on this report. I hope you can help me by providing some contact information."

Professor Morrison was looking uncomfortable. Had she maybe cooked up this report herself?

"Professor Morrison," he pursued, "can you tell me whether this report has more than one author?"

Dan detected the beginning of a blush. Something was definitely going on here. He took out his notepad and a pen. After writing a few lines, he tore off the sheet and handed it across the table.

"Professor Morrison, I would appreciate it if you would give this to whoever gave you that report." He began to stand up and then leaned in confidentially. "I'm so old school, I still use pen and paper. Nobody can tell me that the old methods don't work."

On the paper, he had written his name and phone number, along with a blunt message:

> USG needs to verify the accuracy of your report. Thank you for your cooperation. Noncooperation will be taken as a negative indicator.

"That guy from the Climate office gave me the creeps," Deborah told Wayan, as soon as he walked in the door. "He had eyes that bore holes in you. In books they always call them 'gimlet eyes.'" She handed him the scribbled note and watched his face for a reaction.

"No need to deal with those people anyway," he said, handing the note back. "I've been thinking about maybe getting in touch with the people I worked with last year, at USAID." He heaved his backpack onto the floor. "I think they'll at least be straight with me about what they want to do with the report, if anything." Wayan opened his arms for a hug, and she kissed him.

"The more important question," he said, smiling, "is, what's a *gimlet*?"

Deborah pulled him down onto the bed, laughing. "What's a *cuddle*?" she asked. So they had one.

"Let's get some dinner," she said finally. "There's something I have to show you."

She picked up her laptop bag as they walked out the door. They went to the café up the street, the one close enough to walk to.

"So, what do you have to show me?" he asked, as they walked.

"I have to *show* you, not *tell* you." She squeezed his hand, in the excitement of sharing her secret.

As soon as they had ordered their food — and before they got greasy — Deborah took out her laptop and opened it. She pulled up her journal, almost nervous about sharing it with Wayan.

"I started writing this for myself, after our last conversation at the rice fields. I didn't even think I could share it with you. And then I realized that you are really the person I was writing it for, in the first place."

Wayan took the computer and studied the screen intently. Finally, he handed it back to her. He looked at her eyes, and, smiling, shook his head.

"How did you manage to write all the things I've been thinking?"

Deborah smiled back at him. "I learned from you."

That Saturday was the day they had picked to visit Wayan's family, in the village a few hours outside of Ubud. He was hoping that his married sister would visit as well, bringing the children and maybe her husband, but at least his brother and sister-in-law were sure to be there.

His mother welcomed Deborah with gestures of greeting that needed no translation; Deborah could see instantly where Wayan got his lively eyes. Wayan then brought her into the house, where his father was listening to gamelan on the radio; he immediately stood to greet them, before settling back again. They moved out onto the porch, where his mother was waiting to present two of her grandchildren — Wayan's brother's children, he explained. The children's mother soon joined them, carrying a tray with refreshments, and she urged them, in English, to take their seats. Wayan introduced her to Deborah.

"Lili and my brother take care of everything, the farm and the house. That is why I am able to do my own work."

The children — around six and four, Deborah judged — stood shyly behind their mother. Wayan beckoned them forward and offered them rice cookies from the platter.

"My niece and nephew," he told Deborah. "Although," he reflected, "in Indonesian and Balinese, we don't actually have those words. It's like our word for grandparent — we use the same word for both sexes." The children each took a cookie and quickly went back to their mother, their eyes fixed on the strange visitor. "In fact," Wayan continued, "our traditional names are all for both men and women. What they reveal is birth order, not sex."

Deborah waited until they were back in her room to ask Wayan the question that was occupying her mind. Was his mother okay with their relationship?

"She is very happy to finally see me with someone who makes me happy. I know she has worried about me for years." Wayan looked troubled.

"What's wrong?"

"Deborah, I'm — I'm sorry. I should have brought you to meet my family long ago. I just didn't want to think about how hard it was going to be, to make this fair to you. This can't be just about making me happy. And I was fooling myself into thinking that it will make you happy."

"Maybe I should be the judge of that?" Deborah was starting to feel an old, familiar sense of dread.

"But you don't really know how things are here. I can't see you living Lili's life, and neither can you. Here, the family takes over everything, if you are a woman." He took her hands in his. "I could never deserve that kind of sacrifice from you. From a woman who has so much that is wonderful in her own life."

What was there to say? It didn't take much imagination to see a future of unresolvable tensions with his family, and a weight of guilt on both of them. But for some reason, that sense of dread seemed to dissipate. She knew that she was not imagining the current of electricity flowing between them.

"Let's give it some thought," she said gently. "You are right, we both need to think of the whole picture. Why don't we take a break, just for a couple of days?" She wasn't so clear, right now, about what she wanted herself, despite that undeniable electric current.

But it did not feel good to watch Wayan heading back out the door, half an hour later. At least he didn't pack up his things, just carried his backpack and his phone.

Deborah was still feeling that electricity in her body several hours later, as she tried to fall asleep alone. Was *this* how to figure out what she really wants? By learning that she can't have it? The Romeo and Juliet story still seemed relevant, so many centuries later. The claims of families, all those obligations and anchors, they are very real — even when they are not wielding rapiers.

The morning came upon her like a weight, but she was determined not to mope. So, after a quick breakfast, she arranged with Mario to go back to one of her research sites, even though it was Sunday.

When she got back home it was past four o'clock. Candace emerged at her door to tell her that Wayan had been there. "I was just about to go out for lunch, around 1:00, and he was coming in the gate. I said I thought you'd gone out."

"Thanks, Candace." Deborah made her voice nonchalant, with some effort. Had Wayan come back to see her — or just to get his things? She needed to know; she couldn't know.

Full of purpose, she started the kettle for some tea, and while waiting for it to boil she stretched her body into a downward dog.

Dan's phone conversation with the Deputy Czar is brief. He did indeed meet with *Professor* Deborah Morrison, who looks to be about sixteen years old. She got definitely flustered when he asked about the authors of the meteorological report. It's pretty clear that some bunch of geniuses cooked up this report as a marketing scheme — probably to sell a line of "crystals" from Bali, or what have you. No need for the U.S. Government to help them out; they can make a buck on their own.

His next call will be to Jody, at the Embassy in New Jakarta. Nothing to see here, folks!

He reflects that he probably should have stopped by the USAID office, while he was in NewJak.

The message from Wayan came as Deborah was finishing her tea, having gone through Warrior Two to Triangle (both sides). Spot yoga, she had begun to call it: no fussing with a mat, even.

Making sure to breathe properly, she checked her phone.

> "need to see you – when is good?"

How about now? she thought, and typed:

> "in about an hour"

Not going to fuss. But she did some tidying.

She heard the motorbike pull up right on time — though, to be honest, not a minute too soon. She dispensed with coyness and came out to meet him at the gate. There was no kiss, but a gleam of gratitude, and they walked together to her room. Deborah indicated the two chairs at the table and they sat down.

"Thank you for giving me time to think," he began. "I did a lot of thinking." He took a breath, and Deborah offered to make tea. He took her hand to restrain her.

"Here is what I figured out. Visiting my parents' place, the thing that eats at me is that I have a *house* there."

Deborah felt herself stiffen, suddenly awaiting some finality, and she took back her hand.

"It's not really my house, I've never lived in it. A cousin is staying there. But to my parents, this is the place that I will raise a family — just like my brother."

Wayan closed his eyes for a moment and gave himself a little shake. When he opened his eyes, he was looking at her face.

"Deborah, that is not what I want. It's not just that you can't be Lili. I can't be my brother, either. I just — I was never brave enough to tell them that. Or even to think it."

He looked down and continued to talk, as if to himself. "I haven't lived in the village since I went to Australia for two years. That was only a few months after Dian died. I think I always knew I wasn't coming back home. But not my family. To them, it's only temporary, even after ten years."

Wayan looked up again. "Deborah, I will make this right. I know what I need to do. I need to help them understand that I will be living a different way from them, and that it is not because of you. I am begging you, please — tell me I can come back to you, when I have made amends to my family?"

They didn't see each other for a week. Wayan sent messages at least every day, sounding buoyant, and Deborah tried to keep her mind on other things. She had materials to organize for the semester's classes, as well as a field report to finish. Then, on Sunday morning, he texted to suggest having dinner together. The message made her happy and hopeful. But dinner? This might be a difficult conversation. She messaged him back: how about meeting that afternoon at the ARMA museum, for a stroll around the grounds?

Wayan was waiting near the entrance when she arrived, holding two tickets. He almost ran to meet her and grabbed both her hands. All he said was, "Deborah."

Inside the gate they walked in silence to the large courtyard. Wayan pointed out a bench where they could sit in the shade.

"I have a lot to tell you," he said, as they sat down. Deborah restrained the urge to put her arm around him, sitting so close.

He had begun the discussion by sitting down with his brother and Lili. They were not at all surprised to hear that he was not planning to move back, but they agreed that he needed to discuss it with his parents. His brother advised him to talk to the village priest, who understood a lot more than just the Hindu rituals. It proved to be an excellent suggestion. Wayan asked the priest: Was there a way for him to give his house back to the family, while showing honor and gratitude, with some kind of ritual? And the priest agreed to visit the family and help them do it properly.

But Wayan also wanted to help his family understand that he was still honoring the Balinese traditions, in his work and in his life. And that was what made him think about Deborah's essay, *Earth Logic*. With the help of his brother and Lili, he had translated her words into Balinese.

"My English is much better than theirs, but I'm no longer fluent in Balinese. All my work is in Indonesian and English," he explained. "The amazing thing is, the translation works so well, it's almost as if you must have been thinking in Balinese."

> It took them several hours (he told her), working on Wayan's laptop. Then he had six copies printed up, and he brought one copy with him to give to the priest. He explained to the priest that this had been written, in

127

English, by his American fiancée (and here, Wayan's eyes began to tear up — and Deborah's ears tingled at the word "fiancée"). The priest had taken a few minutes to read the essay, and then he looked at Wayan and said, "Maybe we can create a new blessing, with words from your fiancee's journal." He said he would come to the house that Saturday.

Wayan's brother and Lili were delighted with this plan. They wanted Deborah to be part of the ceremony, but Wayan insisted that this was not about his relationship with her. This was only about his relationship with the *house*. He wanted to make it completely clear to everyone that Deborah had not come between him and his family.

Saturday could not have gone better. The day before, Wayan and his brother had talked with their parents to explain that Wayan needed to give up his claim on the house, because as long as he was working he would be living away from their home. They explained that the priest was coming the next day, to say the needed prayers and blessings. That evening, Wayan's mother and sister-in-law spent hours preparing snacks and sweets for the event.

On Saturday morning, after gathering them all at the family shrine, the priest led some prayers of thanksgiving. He then brought out his copy of *Earth Logic*. He presented it almost as an offering, reading sentence after sentence about the connection between humans and nature. The second part of the ritual took place in front of Wayan's house, where Wayan expressed his gratitude for his home and released his claim on the house.

Now that the ritual was complete, they all gathered on the veranda of the parents' house, where a table had been set up laden with plates of goodies. The priest heaped a plate with assorted snacks, but then he put it aside. He talked about the text he had used for the ritual. He quoted a few more sentences from it, and then he turned to Wayan. Would he please explain to his family how he had obtained this beautiful text?

So Wayan began to talk to his parents about those visits to the rice fields, and the conversations they had about the traditions of honoring the earth and the water. He finished by bringing out copies of *Earth Logic*, in Balinese, to give to each member of the family, and by giving thanks that Deborah had written this journal.

Deborah had listened in silence to Wayan's retelling, keeping her eyes on his face as he spoke. There was no alarm, no apprehension in her: she knew from his first words, as well as from his evident sense of relief, that his mission had been successful. So why, why on earth, was she bursting into tears, just as he finished telling her his story?

Chapter 12

Things were normal again between them. Better than normal. Now, they were truly partners: they had a shared interest, an investment, really, in *Earth Logic*.

And they both felt the daily urgency of simply being together, before Deborah's departure for home.

For Deborah and Wayan, her private journal had already served an important purpose, just by being shared with five important people. But there had to be a wider audience for it, they agreed. So, at Wayan's urging, they decided to upload *Earth Logic* — in both languages — on BasaBali. Wayan seemed to feel his own pride of authorship; he seemed, if anything, more determined to publish it than Deborah.

"Wayan, what about your report?" she asked him. "Not just the chart, but the whole report?"

"You mean, put it on BasaBali?"

Deborah nodded.

Wayan looked thoughtful. "Okay, we upload the report, but without my name on it."

"And we can link it to Earth Logic, okay?"

Cecily phoned as they were going to get some dinner. Deborah put her on speaker.

"Now that we shared *Earth Logic* with Mattias, there's a bunch of other people I want to send it to."

"What did Mattias say about it?"

"He was very positive, in his way. But he said right away, where's the data? I know you told me that Wayan did the basic climate research, and there's a report. Can I give that to Mattias too?"

Wayan immediately shook his head; but then he said to Deborah, "Let's just send them the links on BasaBali."

Deborah promised to send Cecily the link to the report.

"Good, I can look at it tonight. But isn't there a way to get the report *published* — not just have a download somewhere? If it's not published it doesn't really exist. Mattias felt strongly that the data report needs to be out there, before you put *Earth Logic* in front of people. I think he's right."

Deborah had no choice: she had to return to the U.S. The fall semester was starting in two weeks, and there were several tasks that required her to be on campus.

Packing up was a simple matter of just bringing *everything*. She bought an extra bag for the things she had acquired — and especially for her sketches, packed inside the sketchbook. But packing to go home did not have the sense of a welcome return, as she usually felt when wrapping up a research trip. Why did she feel that she was *leaving* home?

And when would she make the trip back to Bali?

Joe meets Godfrey at the squash court. It's been ages since they've had enough time for a squash match. As they change their clothes, Joe asks when he's going to see that climate report on Bali.

"That report? We can't verify it, and no one is even admitting authorship. It's most likely some kind of scam."

"Well, the Embassy is interested in it. They asked whether I had the report." Joe is already picking up his racquet bag. "Why don't I send it over to them? Maybe they can determine authorship."

"Sorry, Joe." Godfrey didn't look up from tying his shoelaces. "We just can't serve as a source for something we can't verify."

Deborah felt like a stranger on campus, in her office, even in her apartment. Every time she heard the clock tower chime, it was with a wave of disappointment that it wasn't the gamelan. In an effort to keep the pieces of her life together, she started to go around her apartment taping all her sketches to the walls — even the bad ones.

She decided to get back to sketching. Getting out the sketchpad, she suddenly realized that she needed to do a picture of Wayan — but it soon became clear that they had neglected to take any selfies at all. All of her photos are "lifies" (the current term for photos of anything that isn't yourself). But there is one photo of the two of them in front of the gate at BaliPark, that was taken at the insistence of their guide. There was a major problem with it, however: Wayan was wearing sunglasses. The whole point was to capture his eyes, after all. Sometimes (she told herself), you just have to get creative.

None of her attempts proved satisfactory, in the end. But she went ahead and taped them all up on the walls.

Deborah persuaded Cecily to come for a weekend. They would have long walks in the fall colors and breathe the crisper fall air. And it would be fun to show her the sketchbook gallery.

It was good to catch up. Cecily wanted to hear all about Wayan, and Bali, and especially Wayan. But somehow their conversations almost always ended with her latest pitch for publishing *Earth Logic*. Cecily had lots of arguments: It was wrong to just bury all that information, and her insights. People should have a chance to think it through for themselves. Besides, anyone who is seriously interested in scientific knowledge can't reject an idea just because it's radically new.

"It's not as if science has everything figured out, Aunt Deb." They were walking to the far end of the campus, where the Agriculture School used to have a dairy. "What about that billion-year-gap that Grandpa likes to talk about, in the

134

geological record?" Cecily was beginning to enjoy her role of career coach.

"And what about Dark Matter — most of the universe is made of some stuff that we don't even know anything about. We should probably call it *Light Matter*." Cecily suddenly stopped walking to face Deborah. "Hey! Maybe Dark Matter is actually *love*!" (said the newlywed).

"Cecily, I really appreciate all your help in thinking this through. But you and I both know that there is no scientific journal that would publish my untested speculations."

"Of course they won't!" Cecily sounded offended. "They are the gatekeepers for the old ideas. You need to get your ideas out directly to the whole world, including the folks who don't read books and articles. Maybe you should serialize your piece on Gram!"

"Right. I suppose I can sign up a decent troll-screening service. But you realize, of course, that this would destroy any possibility of my getting research funding ever again."

"Deborah. Science is a great resource, and it has made a ton of amazing discoveries. Including a few of yours — I especially love *Spindasis vulcanus cecilia*. But here's the point." Cecily stopped to face Deborah.

"Let's be honest. If sharing an important and radical new perspective is something that science can't deal with, maybe you need to start thinking about whether science is really the best way for you to work. I mean, how are you going to feel about documenting the last few butterflies in the Indian subcontinent, knowing that you can't publish the things you learned in Bali?"

"Okay. You're right. So, how do you propose I pay my rent, after this Gram adventure? You may recall that there's no tenure these days."

"I've made some good contacts here, Aunt Deb. Including on the acquisitions side. I think there will be definite interest in your book."

Deborah had a lot to think about. She needed to have lunch with Stefan. He might have some ideas about the possiblity of academic publishing in some form. She took a deep breath and sent him the link for *Earth Logic*.

They met a couple of days later at a popular student lunch spot. Stefan was appreciative, but not encouraging. It was the same basic problem: the meteorological report had not been published, so there's no body of data to discuss.

"More to the point, Deborah — you and I both know that it's basically too late. *Way* too late. What if you could have published this twenty years ago — or even in 2020? And what if the whole world had taken the problem seriously back then?" He gave a short, grim laugh.

"We now have the Human Cost Index to tell us just how many lives and how many square miles are being lost, due to all the 'extra' weather — as if counting them really makes any difference. Anyway," he leaned back in his chair, "the only thing more pointless than *future* science fiction is *past* science fiction."

Changing the subject, Deborah shared Cecily's thoughts about *Light* Matter.

"She's not wrong," Stefan mused. "In science, we need to always keep in mind that, even with the best confirmation, we are always dealing with hypotheses. What the discovery of Dark Matter showed us very clearly, I would say, is that the scientific method at bottom rests on one central, framing hypothesis."

"I'm not following you."

"Our scientific methodology insists that every conclusion must be based on data. But here's the weak link: our data is limited to what we can *see*, one way or another — what we can measure. But the only thing we can sense directly are light waves and sound waves. The other kinds of waves that science has dicovered were found using specialized instruments.

"And then, after many decades of doing science, we discover a mystery phenomenon we call Dark Matter that pervades the entire universe. Even with our most sophisticated instruments, we simply cannot *see* it. We can only see its effects. So, what else are we not seeing? Maybe we are living in the midst of some other kinds of wave, or maybe some kind of field, that we cannot sense."

Stefan stopped to take a bite of his Reuben sandwich. Noticing the way he was holding it, rather tidily, Deborah suddenly recalled, irrelevantly, that Stefan was née Stephanie.

"The basic principle underlying the scientific method is that we have the ability to see. But when we come across evidence of things that we have no way of seeing, we have to go with an approximation of their properties. We cannot see time, but we can use even a simple sand clock to make an approximation. We cannot see Earth's magnetic field, but even a rudimentary compass will react to it." He held up the other half of his sandwich, moving it from side to side like a compass needle. "It's the same with Dark Matter. Astrophysicists need some way to account for Dark Matter in the calculations they make, even though they can't see or measure it directly. Does that mean their calculations are based on guesswork?"

Deborah was trying to absorb this perhaps over-complicated argument. But Stefan wasn't finished.

"I could sit here and come up with some kind of mechanism, some channel, to explain how, by placing an offering on the earth, people might actually be affecting the climate. And of course it would sound like a fairy tale. But a lot of science sounds like a fairy tale — and I don't mean just Dark Matter. Take quantum physics, with all its quarks and colors and quirks. (Just kidding, I made that last one up). Those guys are demonstrating the most *unbelievable* stuff."

"Yes, such as … teleporting people?"

Stefan looked confused and a bit worried. "Are you maybe talking about a *TV show*?"

Deborah laughed. "It's okay, Stefan, I was joking!"

Under Indonesia's new immigration structure, even Indonesians did not automatically qualify for entry into Bali, let alone residency. But the domestic permitting process was on the whole manageable, and Pak Ika himself kept tabs on each residency application. For non-Indonesians, however, there was now a strict quota of tourist visas for Bali, bolstered by strenuous immigration enforcement efforts that included a robust drone detection and management unit. (No wall was necessary, thanks to the ocean.) Residency in Bali was becoming a pipe dream: it was all but impossible for foreigners to get their Greener Card. Pak Ika's office experimented for a few weeks with a foreign lottery system, but it quickly became unmanageable.

Bali finally pulled up the drawbridge.

Deborah was still homesick. The fall colors of Ithaca were inspiring as always, in spite of the dry weather; but her mind kept going back to the Indonesian rice fields. Could she even try to capture their beauty on paper? It was a Sunday, and she decided to take an hour or two away from her course preparation. She had lots of lifies of the rice fields, at different times of day, and she picked out the one that would translate best to black and white. At the end of an hour, she had five more sketches to tape to the wall — more sketches than there was room for, even standing on a chair.

One or two of them gave her some satisfaction. But where was the entrancing silver of the water, in the flooded fields? She wanted to share them with Wayan, but she wasn't sure whether he would appreciate her attempts. "Deborah," she scolded herself, "isn't that what trust means? You *share* things, and you both appreciate sharing them."

She took photos of a couple of her rice field sketches and sent them on WhatsApp, aware that it would be the middle of the night in Bali.

Wayan was back in his own apartment full time now, having had a taste of sharing a home over the past two months. The English language had the perfect phrase: he was feeling *out of sorts*. Even his cup of tea in the mornings had less appeal for him. Sleep tended to be fitful these days.

That night, he woke up startled from a dream that felt as ominous as the one in Kuala Lumpur. He was in a rice field, but instead of the stages of green and gold he saw a huge black and white checkerboard stretched out before him. It was the same familiar black and white checked pattern that would drape every shrine and statue, at the religious holidays; but stretched out as a landscape, it seemed to quench all life. In his dream, he was trying to explain to Deborah that the rice fields themselves are the offering — but she was not there.

He checked his phone: 4 a.m. He might as well get up; it would be light in another hour. He stood up, still holding his phone — and the phone pinged a message. And there it was: Deborah's smiling, spacious, healthy rice field, perfectly timed to drive away the image of that inert black checkerboard in his dream.

Wayan laughed as he clicked her number. And there she was.

"I'm really homesick," she told him.

"So am I," he said. "I need you here."

"Wayan, people are telling me I need to publish *Earth Logic*." She decided not to mention Stefan's name. "But it's the same problem that Mattias was talking about. No one would take it seriously if there isn't some data behind it."

"I've been thinking the same thing, ever since we talked to Cecily. How is she, by the way?"

"She always seems happy. She was here last weekend. She loves my sketchbook gallery."

"I would love to see it! But about the report — I tell you what. There's someone I can talk to at USAID who has always been supportive. I will call him tomorrow and ask him about how to publish the data."

"I love you."

"I love you too."

Wayan reached Greg — USAID environmental program manager for Indonesia — in Papua. Greg explained that he was there to finalize plans for a reef protection project, with Health In Harmony.

"Health In Harmony? I thought they do reforestation."

"You're right. But they do it by working with the local people — and that's what we need, if we're going to restore the reefs."

Greg was planning to be in Den Pasar the following week; they should get together then.

It was 6 am, and Deborah's phone was buzzing on the nightstand. She reached it just in time to click on and hear Stefan saying her name.

"Deborah? Mind totally blown. How soon can you meet me?"

"Give me an hour. Breakfast at the Student Union?"

The cafeteria was almost empty, except for a few students who must have pulled an all-nighter. Stefan immediately launched into his new take on their environmental mystery.

"I'm proposing a completely different way of seeing the data. We've been thinking about our global system. We're asking, how do these local climate data and trends function as a part of the global climate system?"

"Of course. Actually, it's been known for some time that we live on a globe. Things are connected."

"I'm not saying the data's not connected, of course it is. But there may be some *other* connections, other levels to think about. Science has been doing this for decades — finding unexplored physical domains — ever since Einstein." Stefan stared into space and began drumming softly on the table with a spoon. Suddenly he looked down at it.

"This spoon can be described lots of ways — its size, shape, weight; its function; its history of manufacture and use. All of that is part of the picture of a global system of physical objects. But, of course, the physical world is also related to the global climate system."

"Wait a second. Can you just explain what a spoon has to do with climate?"

"I don't mean that the spoon is affecting climate. But the way we see the spoon, the way we experience it, takes place within our climate system. Literally — if you leave it outside, the spoon will get warmer on a hot day, or it can be rained on, frozen, or blown away. Just like anything else in our physical world."

Stefan put the spoon into his yogurt and seemed to forget about it altogether.

"Now, along comes Mr. Einstein, and suddenly the entire global system now fits into some *other* picture. And the spoon has to fit into it, just like everything else we see. Here's what I mean.

"Einstein predicted the existence of a *quantum system* that the physical world inhabits, a system has its own 'climate,' so to speak. And maybe microclimates. Quantum ingredients may or may not have size and weight; they are mainly described in terms of 'strangeness' and 'spin' and other terms that were invented just to talk about how they behave. Stuff we can't see." Stefan disappeared into his own thoughts for a minute.

"Basically, physicists showed us that processes and materials in the subatomic world have their own physics — quantum physics. But guess what? It turns out that we also need quantum theory to understand some interactions in molecular biology."

"So, here's my question. How are *quantum fields* related to what we think of as *global climate*?" The spoon once again became a drumstick.

"Anyway, if that question is worth answering, it might require a whole new line of inquiry. Call it *quantum ecology*. The interface between quantum climate and physical climate."

Now Stefan picked up a paper napkin, holding it open with both hands to represent a horizontal surface.

"Einstein asked us to think of the universe as a kind of elastic sheet, of many dimensions — the time-space continuum. And that theory has totally checked out. The evidence of quantum physics tells us that the universe must have begun as a single point, in the Big Bang, and it continues to expand.

"So now, I'm thinking of quantum ecology as a way to situate human action within this continuous space-time field. I'm thinking of quantum ripples, or nodes, where physical actions are maybe reflected or absorbed. And maybe the particular kinds of human actions that create a quantum response are the ones that persist over long periods of time, in a consistent pattern." Holding the napkin taut, he stretched out his pinky finger to poke it from below, creating a bump on the napkin surface. "Maybe, consistent actions can affect the local elasticity of the quantum field — maybe, it can affect it *in the dimension of time."*

"Wait. Stefan. You're talking about the pattern of humans *placing offerings on the earth?"*

Stefan nodded. He finally grinned.

"And that could have an effect in the dimension of *time?"*

Deborah took a long breath. Stefan studied her face, once again in all seriousness.

"Wow, Stefan, you do have a way of complicating things."

"You're welcome, Deb."

"I mean, *of course* I think it's amazing that you found a way to start making sense of the data. I just mean — I have absolutely no idea how we could even use it."

She was sure she sounded whiny, like a teenager who got the wrong color car on Christmas morning.

"I really didn't expect that you would want to start doing quantum ecology. This is just my long-winded way of saying: *Yes, Deborah, you are still doing science!"*

Deborah felt her brain begin to recover. "So, Stefan, let me understand something. Are you maybe thinking of launching a new field of study?"

"Hmm. Find a few colleagues, find a new job, maybe a grant or two. I guess I would say, probably not." His smile was not one of happiness. "To tell you the truth, Deb, transitions kind of wear me out."

Deborah nodded and half-smiled. "Touché, my friend. But you need to publish this stuff, just as much as I need to publish *Earth Logic."*

"It's hard to explain, but I'm honestly tired of freaking people out."

"Look at it this way, Stefan. You're someone who never had the luxury of thinking *inside* the box. So, that must be part of your genius, now, for seeing things that the rest of us aren't able to see."

Chapter 13

Wayan headed out early for the trip to Den Pasar, Bali's capital, located on the southern shore of the island. He was scheduled to meet Greg at 10 am at his hotel, where they would have breakfast.

After some catching-up preliminaries, Wayan got down to business.

"I'd like your opinion on what I should do with this material." He handed him the report. Greg quickly flipped to the charts at the end.

"The report represents twenty years of rainfall and temperature data, for six locations in Bali. The last two charts show the comparison with other locations in the region — Java, Malaysia, Philippines, Thailand."

"This is impressive. Who funded the monitoring?"

"It's part of an ASEAN project based in Singapore, at National University. The project team there has checked out the monitoring procedure and the findings."

Greg nodded thoughtfully. "Are you planning to present it anywhere? What about the rice conference?"

Wayan looked down. "I was on the panel on irrigation. I can't say anyone was very interested."

Now Greg sat up. "Not interested? After seeing these charts?"

"I don't know what people thought. Probably, they thought I needed lessons in Excel."

"Wayan, I'm pretty familiar with the climate landscape of Bali. The fact is, your results present the same picture that I've been seeing for the past seven years. Of course, you go back a lot farther than I do." He held up the report. "Can I keep this copy?"

Wayan nodded.

Greg flipped back to the title page. "No author. Is that for a reason?"

"Well, if people are going to assume it's bad data, or possibly even made-up data, I wouldn't want my name to be on it."

"Okay. Here's what I want to do. I want to visit the Singapore team and get a feel for the whole project, and of course I'll ask about the Bali data specifically. After that all checks out, would you consider including me as a co-author on the report?"

Wayan's face broke out in sunshine, for the first time since Deborah left for the U.S.

It happens that the Economic Counselor at the Indonesian Embassy is Balinese. Pak Agung (AH-gung) regularly checks the news page of the BasaBali website — especially these days, given the intensity of interest in tourism and immigration to Bali.

One fine morning, Pak Agung comes across two separate (but linked) documents about the Balinese climate phenomenon. One is a meteorological report. He quickly realizes that this must be the same document that the Ambassador has mentioned in senior staff meeting, a document that he had been trying to get from the U.S. Climate Czar.

Pak Agung prints out both reports and takes them into the Ambassador's office, not even bothering to phone ahead.

"Sir, I think I found your Bali report online. No author named."

Ambassador Farid takes the report and looks it over with great interest. "What's the website?"

"It's the wiki, BasaBali. Anyone can upload content."

Farid presses his intercom to ask his office assistant to set up a meeting with the Director of USAID. He looked up at Pak Agung. "Joe is the one who originally told me about the report. He may have some more information on it by now."

Pak Agung hands his boss a second document.

"This is another piece on Bali. It's more of a climate essay than a report, but it was linked to that climate report, on the same website."

Joe Medina comes to the Embassy the next day.

"Thank you for coming over," Farid greets him. "I would have been happy to come to you, you know."

"Nothing I like better than exchanging my own glass office for your elegant ballroom suite!"

As they sat down, Joe referred back to their last conversation:

"I have to apologize, Fred, I don't have that Bali climate report to give you. I can't get it out of Godfrey — they've basically buried it at CC."

"That's okay, Joe, it turns out I have sources of my own." Farid gives him a copy of the report and watches him leaf through its pages. "But you'll notice, there's nothing about an author. No name, no affiliation. Nothing."

Joe looks up. "If it's legitimate, the USAID mission in Indonesia ought to be familiar with it. Let me check with them and get back to you."

"I'd appreciate that. And, Joe, would you happen to know where Godfrey got that report in the first place? He probably wasn't looking at a wiki on Balinese culture."

Joe reflected for a minute.

"He had his people track down the source of the #**bali**okay hullabaloo. He was pretty spooked that his own data was showing the same thing as this social media story — basically, claiming that Bali is still okay. And the source turns out to be some woman professor who studies butterflies."

Farid is starting to add two and two. It is just possible that this professor is the author of the climate essay sitting on his desk — *Earth Logic*. And that person is someone he would be interested in meeting. Seeing that the two documents are linked, she might be able to shed light on where the climate report came from.

"Any chance Godfrey would share contact information for this professor? I might want to invite her for the next roundtable, on the Indonesian climate crisis."

"Sure, good idea. I'll be seeing Godfrey on Sunday, to clean his clock on the squash court."

In just a few days, Joe got confirmation from the USAID team in Indonesia. Yes, they knew the author of the climate report. His name was Wayan Rawoh, and he had done consulting work for them over the years on irrigation. Greg was planning to vet the report itself, whenever he could get over to NU in Singapore.

It was a bit more difficult to get the information he wanted from Godfrey. Apparently, the Czar had shoved the Bali case firmly out of mind. Eventually, Joe managed to get the name of the staffer who had contacted the professor, and she shared the contact information, which Joe immediately passed along to Farid.

Deborah had been keeping a low profile in the entomology department. Her colleagues had shown surprisingly little interest in the butterfly mania, as something inhabiting a parallel universe without any relevance for academic discourse; and she picked up no indication that they associated the episode with her.

Absorbed in her classes and her field results, she had stowed *Earth Logic* on a remote shelf of her mind. So, she was unprepared for a phone call from the Indonesian Embassy.

Pak Agung began by introducing himself as the Economic Counselor at the Indonesian Embassy, in Washington, DC. "And am I talking with the author of *Earth Logic*?"

Deborah's mind quickly retrieved the fact that she had posted her essay on an Indonesian website, and that she had linked it to Wayan's climate report. But she double-checked her memory: no, she had not included her name.

Feeling equal parts flattered and spooked, she affirmed the information.

"The Ambassador has asked me to invite you to meet with him and his senior staff, at your convenience, to give us a private briefing on your observations on climate conditions in Bali." Pak Agung paused. Getting no response from Deborah, who was at that moment rather gobsmacked, he continued.

"Unfortunately, we can only pay speakers' expenses for an event that includes public participation, as part of our diplomatic outreach. I hope you will understand. However, if you prefer to appear at a larger event, we can arrange that, and then we would then happily cover the cost of your transportation and hotel."

Deborah asked for a day to consider the invitation. As soon as she hung up, she phoned Stefan. What did he think about this idea, and would he come with her if she went? His analysis would be of much more interest than hers. Stefan was clear: keep it small, just the Embassy officials, but go ahead and do it.

"It's worth the time and money," he pointed out, "just to start bringing the different parts of your brain together."

Traveling together to D.C. gave Deborah and Stefan ample time to talk about what they wanted to say in their presentation. They continued the conversation over lunch at an Asian fusion restaurant on Dupont Circle, just before the afternoon meeting. Deborah was focusing intently on Stefan's latest idea. He took out a pad of graph paper.

"Think of a field. Assume that the rice field that you see co-occurs with another kind of field — one that we can't see. I don't mean the earth's magnetic field, but maybe some kind of quantum energetic field." He sketched a loose rhomboid. "Is it possible that each offering, placed on the ground, creates a *node* in that energetic field? Does the resulting network somehow stabilize the eco-quantum field?" He added some bumps to the rhomboid, to represent nodes in a network.

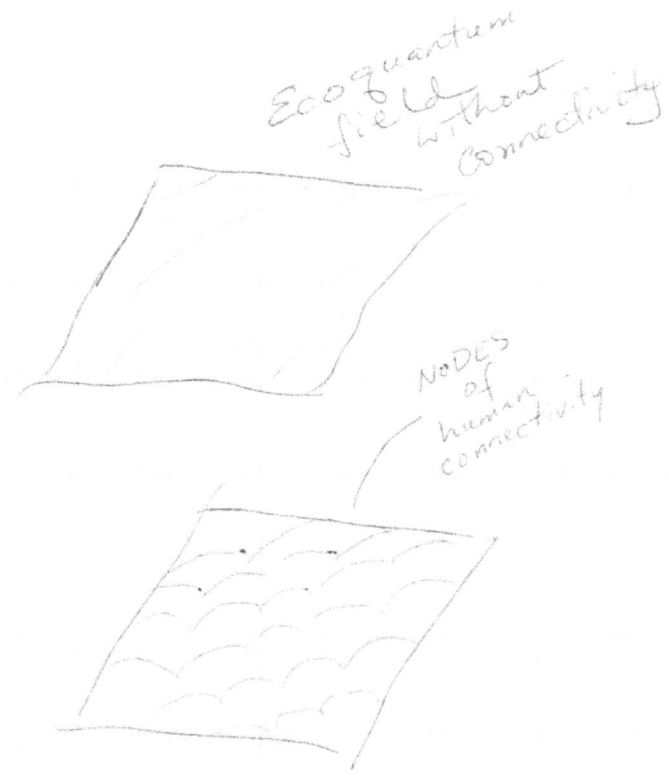

Eco quantum field without connectivity

NODES of human connectivity

"If so – what are the properties of the offering that interact with the quantum field? What makes an offering different from, say, a *suitcase* that you put on the ground?" He started to draw a suitcase and stopped himself, with a sheepish laugh.

"Is it possible that *human intention* is somehow transmitted to the field? And then, how does the eco-quantum field interact with earth's atmosphere? Is *time* the mediating factor? Is it possible that changes at the molecular level are suspended, or even reversed, in the dimension of time?" They both shrugged, simultaneously.

"I told you it would sound like a fairy tale!"

Pak Agung met them when they arrived in the security annex and escorted them into the Embassy building. Following instructions, they stowed their phones in small individual lockers, to which they kept the unwieldy keys. Passing by the security desk and the glassed-in conference room, they proceeded through a corridor into the stately historic mansion.

Pak Agung Deborah and Stefan to two of maybe ten huge mahogany chairs, arranged around a huge mahogany table, in a huge mahogany-panelled room. A glass of water had been set at each place.

"Twenty years ago, I'm told," Pak Agung commented, "these would have been individual plastic bottles!"

Deborah took this as hyperbole, and she gave a polite laugh. She glanced over at Stefan, who seemed utterly unfazed by the imposing setting. Several men and women, smart in their batiks, began to trickle into the room without pausing their conversations. A few stopped to greet the visitors with a handshake; others gave a friendly nod of the head.

The Ambassador entered on time, accompanied by another official (who soon turned out to be the Deputy Chief of Mission). He came over to Deborah, who stood to meet him.

"Welcome, and thank you for taking the trouble to come and talk to us. We are all very interested to hear about your observations."

Deborah introduced Stefan, who was standing next to her.

"Please, everyone, take your seats." As the scraping of heavy chairs subsided, Ambassador Farid asked the staff around the table to introduce themselves. Pak Agung meanwhile distributed copies of *Earth Logic*.

The Ambassador then began the discussion by talking about his own reaction to finding this very absorbing discussion of the Balinese climate phenomenon — especially because it appeared in tandem with the actual climate data. And he quoted from *Earth Logic*:

> The opposite of complaining about the weather is not "doing something about it." The opposite of complaining is *honoring*: honoring the air we are privileged to breathe, the water that sustains us, the earth we inhabit.

Deborah felt a blush coming on. Luckily, she had prepared what she wanted to say.

"Thank you, Mr. Ambassador." She had made sure to ask Pak Agung about the correct form of address.

"Please, call me Farid."

"Thank you, Farid." Was she blushing more, now? "It's a real pleasure to share my thinking with this group of people, who have a serious interest in the impacts of climate change."

She began her presentation with a short account of coming across the chart showing Balinese climate trends, immediately after seeing photographic evidence of an unanticipated butterfly survival in Bali.

"I could find no field research on this particular butterfly, or any related species, in Bali. That was why I funded my own research trip last summer, to try to document this survival. And indeed, I had no trouble finding specimens of this species, as well as many others." She paused for a drink of water. The whole table was paying close attention as she resumed.

"Since you have already read *Earth Logic*, I don't need to tell you that I learned much more during that trip than just about butterfly sightings. The thing that most impressed me was

155

learning about the daily religious practice of placing an offering on the earth. This practice is not just widespread — it is almost universal in Bali, at every home and every shop. And, maybe especially, at the rice fields."

She turned to Stefan. "My colleague has been doing some serious and very creative thinking about this puzzle, and I managed to persuade him to share his thinking with you as well."

Stefan, too, began by quoting *Earth Logic*, calling it his "jumping-off point."

> The almost unchanging climate on the island of Bali presents a challenge to our models of the environment. We already know that our environment includes things we can't yet measure directly, such as the mysterious property called Dark Matter.

He looked around to see that people were following the argument, and he continued to read:

> One possible explanation is that our environment includes some kind of **energy field** that can be affected by even small-scale human activities, performed by thousands of people over the centuries.

"As I've been saying for months to Deborah, just because something sounds like a fairy tale doesn't mean it's not a scientific hypothesis worth exploring. Einstein's space-time continuum is almost impossible for us to imagine or believe in, but it resulted in a century of important work."

Stefan continued to talk about the possible directions for analysis of the Balinese phenomenon, including proposing the new field of quantum ecology — until even he could see that eyes were glazing over.

Then there were comments and questions from around the table, mostly directed to Deborah. Ambassador Farid read another passage from *Earth Logic* that (he said) raised the most provocative questions:

> The most intriguing possibility is that these effects, created by consistently performed activities, may depend on an additional variable: **the factor of human intention**.

He turned to Stefan. "Can you sketch for us some way in which this subjective factor could affect objective climate conditions?"

Stefan looked thoughtful. "It's difficult to even envision the kind of study that we could use to test this variable. You would have to have participating subjects on two similar islands — maybe, Flores and Ambon? — and have them all perform the same physical actions. But the participants on one island are encouraged to include a personal prayer. But even then, who knows how long the experiment would need to continue before you could expect to see some effect?" Stefan shook his head. "We're stuck in the realm of conjecture, on this. And honestly, the way I see it, if human intention is a factor, we should probably just go back to studying the writings of the Buddhists and the yogis."

Farid smiled broadly as he stood up. He walked around the table to personally thank his special guests, to a round of applause. As the gathering broke up, he invited Deborah and Stefan into his office for a cup of coffee.

"Sumatran, not Balinese," he joked. Pak Agung joined them, as they took their seats around the Ambassador's coffee table.

"Agung tells me that this is actually the first time for you to present Earth Logic to an audience."

Deborah nodded, "That's right."

"It seems to me," Farid continued gently, "that this is an important line of inquiry, for literally everyone on Earth. It needs to be shared. Do you have plans for publication?"

Deborah shook her head. She explained that although she had been discussing how to publish, there was one major difficulty. Until the climate data could get published in some recognized channel, she saw no chance whatsoever for *Earth Logic* to be taken seriously.

As soon as Greg learned that the Director himself had been asking about the Bali climate report, he wasted no time in getting himself over to Singapore to conduct his due diligence inquiry. A meeting with the ASEAN project team quickly confirmed Wayan's account. The team's monitoring specialist had assisted Wayan with his setup and had checked his findings, more than once. The team had no reason not to trust his reported results.

Greg filed a trip report with the USAID Indonesia mission, who immediately forwarded it to Washington to the attention of the Director, who got on the phone to the Indonesian Ambassador.

"Fred, I have the mission findings on the Bali climate report. It does check out. Our guy met with the project team at NU, and they have confidence in the report."

"Thanks, Joe, this is important information," Farid replied. "So, tell me, are you planning to publish the report?"

"It's not ours to publish, Fred. We didn't contract it."

"So, that means no one will publish it?"

There was a bit of silence on the phone line.

"I see what you mean. I will talk to the ASEAN office about doing a partner contract, just on the deliverables."

158

"Excellent! This is important data. I know this is preaching to the choir — but we are suffering on so many fronts. Flooding, wildfires, unpredictable rainy season, it's all getting worse every year." Farid's voice went quieter. "They tell me we might have to give up growing coffee and tea altogether."

"Believe me, I know. It's been a catastrophe for Indonesia."

"So, to me, the idea of burying this climate data — it just shocks the soul. And, Joe, in my view, we will just have to manage the PR consequences."

Greg's number came up on Wayan's phone — after Deborah's, the number he most wanted to see.

"Wayan, things are looking good."

"Yes, you told me you had a good visit to the team in Singapore."

"It gets better than that. USAID Washington wants to publish your report! It will be a partner document with ASEAN. So, I don't think you need any co-authors on this."

"Do you think this is definite, or just a possibility?"

"It's from the top guy. I guess my word counts for something after all."

"Greg, I owe you a lot. I hope I get a chance to host you properly, soon."

"I'm just happy to see a good outcome for a good report. I'll give your number to the publications office. They will need you to sign a contract, probably sell them the copyright. USAID only publishes reports it has contracted for."

Almost before they ended the call, Wayan was phoning Deborah. It was evening over there.

"Deborah, the report is going to be *published*! As a USAID report — so it might get some serious attention."

Wayan can hear Deborah jumping up and down and wooting.

When she got back on the phone, he continued. "The only thing is, I am giving them the copyright. It's how they do publications. That means, we won't be able to publish it as a package with *Earth Logic*."

"You sure you're okay with that?"

"You mean, the copyright? I am just so happy it will finally get out. So now we just need to figure out how to publish *Earth Logic*."

Deborah's first instinct was to call Stefan, to find out what he could tell her about the USAID process.

"Deborah, that's great! It's not a scientific peer-reviewed journal, of course. But USAID publications are solid, field-based research. And these days, they are known for getting good results on the ground as well. They've been empowering women in the past couple of decades, and it has made a lot of difference. It's a good brand."

"But how long will it take, do you think? To get published?"

"If it's already cleared in Washington, could be just a few weeks."

Deborah sat and breathed. Relief flooded around her like a brain massage. Relief that Wayan's work was being appreciated, and that he sounded so happy. But also — and maybe even bigger — relief that the world was working the way it should. That this important information would become widely known, instead of ignored.

So now, what about her own work? When it seemed that Wayan's report would be permanently shelved, she didn't have to think about what to do with *Earth Logic*. After all, her essay was written as a meditation on the baffling real-world phenomenon that his report described. Without that report, it would be just a meditation on a social media hashtag.

But if the essay made no sense without the climate report, it was equally true that the report didn't really make sense without all the detailed background exploration she had gathered into *Earth Logic*.

Deborah took a deep breath and phoned Cecily.

It was late in the evening, and Cecily was finally getting a chance to try on her new foldable bike helmet. She took it off to answer the phone.

"Aunt Deb! Are you snowed in up there?"

"Kind of. I'm not driving anywhere, that's for sure. I can think of places I'd rather be."

Cecily laughed. "I bet."

"I have really good news. USAID is going to publish Wayan's report! He says it's definite."

"Wow, that's amazing! It will be up on their website, that means." Cecily put down the helmet and sat on the arm of the sofa. "So, let's strategize. We can be ready to roll as soon as his report is released."

Here is what they came up with.

Earth Logic would be serialized on Reedy. Each slice of the essay would come with an embedded hologram illustration — one of Deborah's sketches. They would get permission to insert links to the USAID report. *Earth Logic* episodes could be shared all kinds of ways, but without the hologram. The idea was to go viral, and also attract subscribers.

And viral it went. . . .

Episode 1

**The Balinese people
have always kept a careful
balance in their
relationship
with the earth.**

**Each day, at every doorway,
they place an offering on the
earth.**

**They have done this for
hundreds, or maybe thousands,
of years.**

***And the earth
reciprocates.***

Wayan was even more excited to see Earth Logic episodes than he had been to see his own report published on the USAID website. He got subscriptions for almost everyone he knew, and the first one was for Teresa Campbell.

The most intriguing episodes, for him, were the ones that had to do with quantum ecology — material he hadn't seen in Deborah's early draft. He called her early in the morning; it would be around dinnertime there, he guessed.

"Deborah, your book just gets better and better. I wish you were here, so we could be reading each episode together."

"Me too, I keep trying to see things through your eyes, but it's not easy."

"How did you start thinking about ecology in a quantum dimension?"

After a slight pause, Deborah answered, "Actually, that whole idea came from Stefan. Remember, he's the one that never thinks inside the box."

Another pause.

"Wayan, you definitely do not have anything to worry about. I only see Stefan for his professional opinion. I've barely even talked to him since *Earth Logic* came out."

"He sounds like a very interesting person. I wish I could meet him."

"I wish you could, too. It's a bit like talking to Teresa, you never know what he's going to come up with."

When a thing goes viral, it can have some strange side effects.

A lot of literal-minded folks began to adopt the practice of placing a daily offering on the ground. So now, there were blogs and videos and even some in-real-life classes to show you how to weave the little offering basket (substituting parchment paper for the coconut leaves, though you could also buy those online). When Deborah was asked in an interview about this craze, she had her answer ready.

"The key ingredient of the Balinese offering seems to be devotion. The offering goes along with a deep respect for the natural world, and that's more important than the basket."

Cecily immediately tweeted out her own, saltier opinion: "So, if you rape the earth and *then* give it an offering, does that make the earth a *prostitute*?"

Deborah was getting good at doing interviews. She began to get speaking invitations, some of which paid quite well. Most surprising, to her, were the invitations to participate in academic symposia, on topics such as "the inherent problematic of observation, as the basis of scientific method."

Cecily huffed into the doorway, practically throwing her backpack onto the tiled floor. Mattias poked his head out of the kitchenette, where a plate of nachos waited on the counter for a last, lavish topping of sliced jalapenos.

"What's good?" he grinned, wiping his hands with a dishtowel.

"That *TOAD*!" Cecily tore past him and landed heavily on the sofa, as if crushing an enemy. "So, this is the same guy who spouts off that there's no 'common good' anyway, it's just a socialist myth to stomp on his God-given individual rights. And now, guess what?" She stood up ready to take the mic. "Now, it's those ame *socialist elites* that have trashed the planet! As if he has a right to be angry at anybody — as if he ever lifted a finger to do anything about it." She sat down again, as if depleted. "I bet even his beer cans go into the trash."

As if on cue, Mattias placed two beers on the coffee table as he took a seat, giving Cecily's scowling forehead a quick kiss. "Hey, now. People have a right to feel bitter at all the snowbirds and the 'Bali birds' who can afford to get the hell out."

This did not have a soothing effect on Cecily, who again jumped to her feet.

"Oh, right, you're three years older than me so you get to mansplain everything! I'm 30, and I definitely remember the climate wars. There was massive who-the-hell-cares, everybody has a right to guzzle and pollute. And now this creepo is yelling that *somebody else* was supposed to take care of stuff — so we can all drive a truck to the store!"

"I don't mean that his argument is right. Obviously, he is not looking in the mirror." Mattias carefully picked up his beer. "I just think — being angry is kind of a basic right. Most of us aren't too careful about picking the right people to be angry at."

"Oh, okay. Nicely played, sir! I get it, *everybody has a right to be angry except me!*"

Even as she said the words, Cecily was struck by her own acid tone. How had this escalated so fast? Overwhelmed by fury and mortification, with a muttered, "Excuse me," she abandoned the field.

Sitting in the bathroom and fighting off a total meltdown (and multitasking, naturally), she tried to turn her brain back on. It took her a few minutes, and more than a few yoga breaths, but it did begin to work. She went back to the sofa, where Mattias had been making some inroads into nachos and beer.

"I'm sorry, Matty, I didn't mean to snap at you. This whole day feels like my bike just got sideswiped — on purpose." She sat

165

down again. "You can't even argue with this guy. Anything you say, he just drops it into the big box labeled, 'Stuff-I-don't-listen-to.'"

Mattias had apparently done a bit of thinking as well. All he said was, "That really sucks."

"I didn't even tell you the worst part. Phil tells everyone that *Earth Logic* is a big, fat, self-indulgent snowflake. By some star worshipper. Selling a line of crystals."

"I doubt he even read it, you think?"

"That's still not the worst part, though. The worst part is what I said."

"Which is?"

Cecily picked up her beer and then put it down, without taking a sip. "Mattias — *I* didn't actually say *anything*. What the hell is wrong with me? I know what I think, I just don't have the guts to say it!"

"We both know you have plenty of guts, kiddo. Maybe, you're just too thoughtful to lash out at people without thinking everything over." Finishing his beer, he looked up and grinned. "Except *maybe* once in a while."

Cecily made a face at him, and then burst out laughing. She scooted sideways to sit next to him on the sofa, and reached over and grabbed his head for a kiss. "I am *soooo* lucky to have you!"

Then she grabbed the plate from the table and leaned back into the curve of his outstretched arm.

"Good nachos, babe." She chewed in thoughtful silence.

"Too much jalapeno?"

"No, no, it's fine! I was just thinking." Cecily leaned forward to pick up her beer, then stopped and looked back at him.

"You remember *avocados*?"

Deborah's professional life had been transformed. Her department granted her a semester's leave, to accommodate her schedule of public speaking and media appearances.

But her private life now revolved around an inconvenient truth. There were no longer any visas to Bali, if you were not Indonesian. None. Nada. And Bali is where she needed to be.

That was why she was especially pleased to receive an email from Ambassador Farid himself, asking her to suggest possible dates when she might be available to participate in a public forum at the Embassy. There could be no one better, she felt, to consult on this dilemma.

It turned out to be a beautiful spring day in Washington when she arrived at the Embassy. A poster outside announced the event: "Earth, Water, and Bali."

The security guard at the entrance gate immediately phoned his office, and Pak Agung showed up with a big smile to escort her inside. He brought her directly into the Ambassador's office.

Farid got up from his desk and met them at the door, to show them to some seats around a coffee table. On the coffee table were a couple of stacks of the printed book, to be distributed at the forum.

"Professor Morrison, you are to be congratulated. Your book is not only successful, it is enlightening. You have had a real influence on how people are speaking about the environment."

Deborah smiled her appreciation. "I'm afraid that would be too much to ask of people. But please, just call me Deborah."

"I only wish we had planned a series of these events — we had to limit registration to 200, and we had over 500 inquiries.

Maybe we can get you back some time to speak at a fundraiser, perhaps for rainforest conservation."

"It would be an honor," she said. "And there is something I have been wanting to ask you as well." The old Deborah was impressed with the new Deborah's moxie.

"I'm sure you saw the effect of the #baliokay posting, on the flow of tourism and immigration," she began. "No one could be surprised that Indonesia had to put in place severe limits. And by now, it is impossible even to apply to enter Bali."

Farid nodded. "It's a painful and, we hope, temporary measure."

"Ambassador Farid, I have both professional and personal reasons for wanting to return to Bali. I would very much appreciate any help you could give me."

The ambassador looked thoughtful. "Deborah, I can think of no visa case more reasonable or appropriate than yours. But the truth is, those decisions do not go through the Embassy, they are handled independently by the Consular office. And for Bali, even *they* do not operate with any area of discretion anymore." He looked into the distance as he spoke. "I do think that the Foreign Ministry needs to get more involved at the policy level, and I will be having some discussions with them in the next couple of weeks." He turned back to Deborah. "I will definitely keep your situation in mind."

Farid picked up one of the books from the stack on the coffee table. "I will make sure to have copies of this book to share at the Ministry as well." He smiled. "It occurred to me, as I read your book, that the Indonesian term for 'homeland' means, literally, 'Earth and Water.'"

It was a month later that Deborah received an email from the Consular Department of the Indonesian Embassy. She was invited to call to set up an interview appointment at the New York City Consular Office; the email included a confirmation code. When she called the phone number, a woman came on the line and asked her for the confirmation code. Apparently this code was some sort of magic, like "Open Sesame." Deborah could hear the smile on the other end of the line.

"Professor Morrison, I am pleased to inform you that you are eligible to apply for a new category of visa for Bali. It is called *Earth Ambassador*. I can send you the application by email. Now, may I set up an interview appointment for you?"

As soon as the call was finished, Deborah phoned Wayan. She could hear pure, joyful relief in his voice — the voice that went right through her and deep inside, down to her toes.

For Pak Ika, the new visa category came as a pleasant surprise. Like all the longer-term visas, an Earth Ambassador would require an in-person interview with the sponsoring agent. He always enjoyed that part of the process — and the banjars, who profited nicely from these sponsorships, were always appreciative of his services. Looking around his small and slightly shabby office, he wondered how he might manage to obtain an upgrade.

When the first Earth Ambassador application landed on his somewhat cluttered desk, Pak Ika gave it careful scrutiny. The sponsoring banjar was not one of the regulars; in fact, he had not heard of it before now. The signature in the co-signer space was equally unfamiliar to him. He marked the box for his assistant to schedule an interview, checking it as "priority."

So it was only a few days later that Dr. Wayan Rawoh appeared at the door of Pak Ika's small office and was invited to take the chair opposite his desk.

"I see that you are personally sponsoring this application for an Earth Ambassador visa."

"Yes, Pak."

"You understand, I'm sure, that this is a very special category of visa. It even allows for an unlimited number of extensions."

"Yes, Pak."

"So naturally, we need to be very careful in how we grant these particular visa applications." Pak Ika held Wayan's gaze for a long minute. "We need to be sure not only about the applicant, but also about the *sponsors*." Another long pause.

"Yes, Pak, I am sure that you will find I have an excellent record. I am an active member . . ."

Pak Ika's stare became impatient. He touched his mustache for reassurance. "Of course, of course. But you will need to have some positive relationship *with this office* as well."

"Yes, Pak, whatever information you need . . ."

This was becoming exasperating for Pak Ika, who was used to dealing with more knowledgable individuals. Wayan — who was, in truth, more used to dealing with international aid agencies — barely spoke the language.

"I have plenty of *information*! But we must be very, very strict about limiting our immigration." Now he reached into his top desk drawer and brought out his favorite prop — a chart, laminated for frequent use. "You can see the big picture here," he began his standard lecture. "This orange line shows just how special the island of Bali has become. And if the trend continues, I expect that the whole world will be coming to my office!"

Wayan was too startled to be able to form a proper sentence. What he blurted out was, "*My chart!*"

"Excuse me, sir. This is most definitely *my* chart, printed up by my assistant in large format."

"No, of course, I'm sorry, Pak. What I mean is, it's my *data*. The chart is from my report for the Conference on Rice Agriculture in Southeast Asia." Wayan sat back in his chair. "It shows the *Meteorological Trends for Bali in the Context of Southeast Asia Weather Patterns, 2016-2036.*"

Now Pak Ika took another long minute, staring at Wayan's face. An amazing new idea was forming. This chart — *his* chart . . . .

Gratitude was suddenly beginning to run in the other direction. Not only on account of this very useful laminated chart, but also for the new position itself. His new title. This very fertile field of endeavor.

Pak Ika was not an ungrateful man. He stood up, finally, beaming at his new-found friend. He reached out his hand across his desk.

"Mr. Rawoh, you are to be congratulated. It is an honor for me to personally award your friend the first Earth Ambassador visa!"

Arriving for the second time at the airport in Den Pasar felt very different. Deborah hoped that no one would recognize her, from all the interviews and book talks that had been posted on WeTube. Naturally, she was disappointed when nobody did.

But stepping out of the terminal felt like coming home — into air that was still fresh with oxygen, and light that was still filtered through green.

And, beyond the security fence, she knew, there would be Wayan.

Epilogue

Like so many others, you and I are waiting to see whether the principles of *Earth Logic* can catch on as a way of seeing the world.

Cynicism, after all, has had a good long run.

It is just possible that something may have indented the time dimension of the time-space continuum. If that is the case, you might actually be reading these words back in the 2020s, or even earlier.

I like to think that every book is a "choose your own ending" story, since the author has to stop writing somewhere. But maybe, if the time dimension has shifted — if you are reading this book 25 years ago, in, say, 2022 — this story can be a "choose your own beginning." And maybe the world can be a better living space for everyone.

One thing is clear. We will not *all* be able to fit in the small island of Bali.

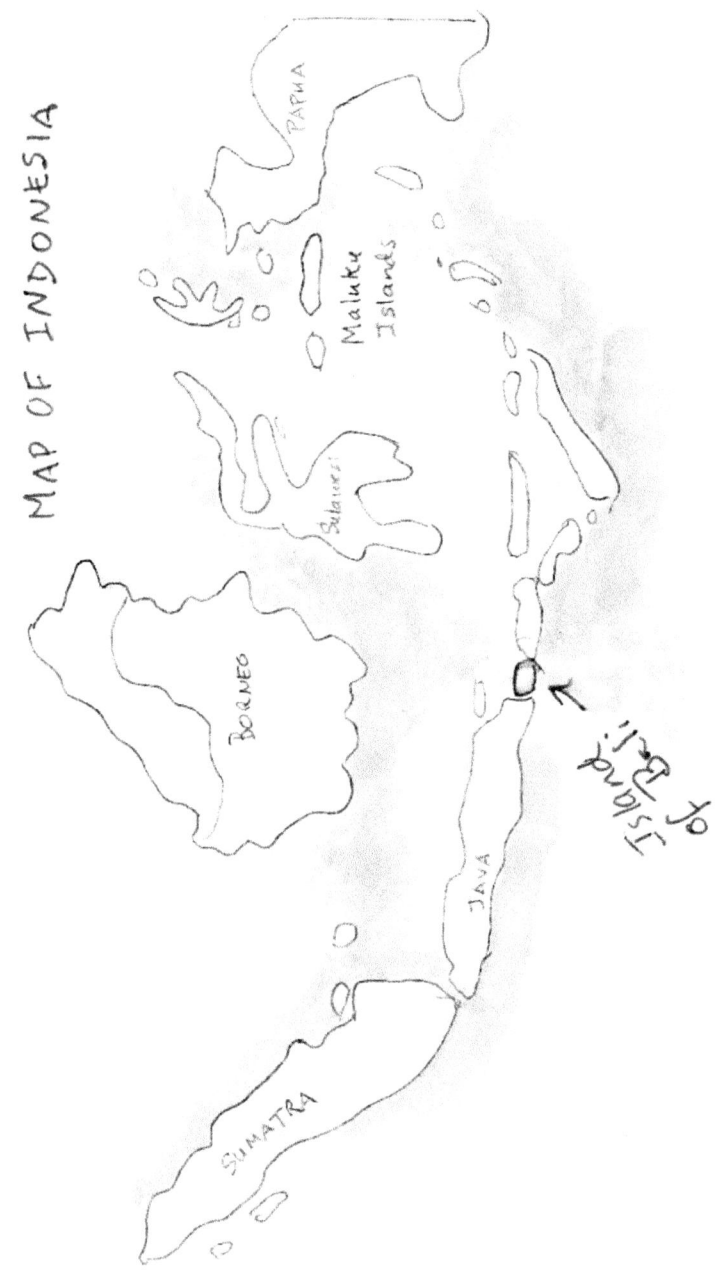

MAP OF INDONESIA

PAPUA

Maluku Islands

Sulawesi

BORNEO

JAVA

Island of Bali

SUMATRA

175

All proceeds from the sale of this book
go to support the work of
Health In Harmony
and partner non-profit organizations.

Health In Harmony is a pioneer
in community-based environmental protection
working in Indonesian Borneo,
Madagascar, and Brazil,
to empower local communities to
protect and restore their forests.

To learn more about this multi-faceted
conservation program, please visit
www.healthinharmony.org.

Synopsis

Bali OK is a love story woven around the theme of climate change. *Bali OK* is also a scientific mystery story, with a twist — and with a chaser of hope.

In the year 2037, climate change has become an undeniable fact of life. Amazingly, one tiny piece of the planet has remained unchanged: the island of Bali. When social media discovers Bali's thriving butterflies, a flood of the world's more affluent immigrants seek out Bali's throwback climate, pursuing the visa that people call the "Greener Card."

Two scientists independently become aware of this anomaly: Deborah, an American a butterfly scientist, and Wayan, a Balinese agricultural scientist. Their search for a scientific explanation soon brings in Deborah's colleague, Stefan (who, as a transgender man, has always had to think outside boxes). Stefan sketches out for them a new theory he calls *quantum ecology.*

Bali OK gives an anthropologist's view of the age-old culture of Bali, enlivened by Deborah's pen-and-ink sketches. Underlying the narrative is a recurring theme around the importance, and the challenges, of sharing knowledge.

The reader will come away with a smile — and with a new sense of the possibilities for navigating our next global challenge.